Another Sad Day
at the Edge of the Empire

STEPHEN GUPPY

Another Sad Day at the Edge of the Empire

OOLICHAN BOOKS
Lantzville, British Columbia
1985

ISBN 088982-061-9 (Hardbound)
ISBN 088982-060-0 (Softbound)

Canadian Cataloguing in Publication Data

Guppy, Stephen, 1951-
     Another sad day at the edge of the empire

ISBN 0-88982-061-9 (bound). — ISBN
     0-88982-060-0 (pbk.)

I. Title.
 PS8563.U66A82 1985   C813'.54   C85-091227-X
PR9199.3.G86A82 1985

48,421

Publication of this book has been financially assisted by the
Canada Council.

Published by
OOLICHAN BOOKS
P.O. Box 10, Lantzville, B.C. V0R 2H0

Printed in Canada by
MORRISS PRINTING COMPANY LTD.
Victoria, B.C.

for Jerry and Thora Howell
and for Nelly, of course

ACKNOWLEDGEMENTS

Grateful acknowledgement is made to the following publications which first printed the stories specified:

"A Rural Tale," "A Portrait of Helena Leafly, With Bees," and "Another Sad Day at the Edge of the Empire" have been published in or will be published by *Canadian Fiction Magazine.*

An earlier version of "The Catch" appeared in *The Malahat Review.*

"The Tale of the Ratcatcher's Daughter" appeared in *Rainshadow: Stories From Vancouver Island,* ed. by Ron Smith and Stephen Guppy, published by Oolichan Books and Sono Nis Press, 1982.

The author would like to thank Ron Smith, Geoff Hancock and Carol Windley for their advice on the preparation of the final manuscript of this book.

Contents

The Catch   9

A Portrait of Helena Leafly, With Bees   26

A Rural Tale   38

Ichthus   52

The Tale of the Ratcatcher's Daughter   75

Calm Creek   84

Another Sad Day at the Edge
   of the Empire   100

The Catch

Walleye Jackson was a man embittered. You could see that as easy as anything, just to look once at him, wasting his time as he did every morning God sent him, scuttling over the duck-walks and plankways he'd spun like a spider to cover the mud from his barn to his shack to the sheds and the lean-tos that reared up like fungus all over his farm. It wasn't as if he was busy; there was bugger-all to do on a stump ranch like that. But it wasn't the farm work that kept Walleye stuck in a dither from morning till sunset till Christ-only-knows how far into the night. It was genius.

Walleye Jackson had a mission in life. One thing and one thing only concerned him from the moment he dragged his ass out of his camp cot and staggered downstairs in his grease-spattered longjohns cursing and kicking at dogs to the horrible nights he spent tossing and turning and waking up screaming to scribble down notes on his endless succession of nocturnal visions and dreams. It was flight.

He was going to fly. In the depths of his being, in the marrow of his bones, from the day of his birth he had known it. The problem, of course, lay in finding out *how*. As a child back in England he had leapt off rooftops, out of windows and trees, over cliffs and off bridges. By the time he was twelve, he had already broken every bone in his body. Whole years of his boyhood crept past in a black fog of ether and pain.

As Walleye grew older, his ambition remained undiminished, though his methods began to evolve and mature. Rather than simply hurling himself, mindless of consequences, from the nearest available precipice in the vain hope that some bored and magnanimous deity might look down and, grasping the nature of his predicament, miraculously equip him with feathers and wings, Walleye endeavoured to compensate for his Creator's deplorable lack of foresight by attempting to remodel the equipment at hand.

To this end, he announced the intention of pursuing a career in medicine. His family, delighted to learn that their sullen, intractable heir, who had hitherto displayed no inclination toward any known field whatsoever, had at long last come to his senses and decided to at least make a show of attempting to attain a respectable position in life, consented at once to his plans and lost no time in bundling him off to a modest but reputable college of medicine. There followed, in the lives of his long-suffering relatives if not in his own, a period of blissful and welcome tranquillity. This idyllic interlude was all too soon shattered by the discovery in Walleye's quarters of a cadaver which some days earlier had gone missing from the hospital morgue and which had somehow acquired, in the course of its travels, a huge pair of half-decayed wings.

The result of this episode was that Walleye was handed his hat and a ticket—one way—to the Colonies. Why he chose to go to, of all places, the rain-soaked and desolate west coast of Canada, or for that matter how he had gotten there, was something that Walleye could never entirely remember. Certain things lurked in the back of his mind, to be sure: sea birds and sailing ships, carved nymphs on bowsprits, cabbages and kings. But the rest of his journey was a watery haze. Anyway, there he was, flat on his ass in the middle of nowhere with a cheque every month in the mail from his parents and an undying passion for flight.

He didn't do badly by it, all things considered. Instead of just pitching himself off a cliff (of which, for a change, there were plenty), he settled right in and signed up to work in the bush. Logging agreed with him, oddly enough. When he wasn't out busting a gut on some snow-covered sidehill, he'd hunker down next to the pot-bellied stove in the bunkhouse and lecture the other loggers, most of whom didn't speak very much English, on the technical niceties of aerodynamics.

Walleye's career as a logger came to an abrupt end one

cold afternoon when, while describing the shape of a hawk's wing to a newly-hired chokerman, a delicate Chinaman sporting a long braided pigtail, a cable snapped downhill and, howling past Walleye, whipsawed the little man neatly in half. Walleye was packed up and halfway to Vancouver by the time they'd collected the pieces for burial. Along with the rest of the garbage he took with him in his gunny sack (bird bones and so forth) was a fat wad of dog-eared Canadian dollars, the money he'd saved from his months in the bush. There was more than enough there for Walleye to realize his latest ambition. He was going to purchase a farm.

It wasn't, of course, that he intended to turn into some sort of salt-of-the-earth immigrant sodbuster, communing with nature and making his way by the sweat of his brow. The earth, in fact, was the farthest thing from his mind at the time. What he wanted was an oasis, a hideaway in which he could withdraw from the world while he embarked on a rigorous, disciplined study of all things on God's earth that fly. Somewhere, he reasoned, in the endless, unreadable cabala of feathers and tendons and muscles and claws that he hungrily, desperately carved from bodies of birds of every conceivable species, of eagles and petrels, of falcons and gulls, of sparrows and wood doves and finches and crows, of dream birds and shadow birds, of angel birds trailing the rays of the cold stellar wings, was the answer, the key that would unlock the infinite clockwork of heavenly spheres, that would vanquish the demons of metals and ores, that would wither the root and the seed of the death that was branching and vining inside him from out of the dark, geological core of the earth. He would build himself laboratories, austere halls of science, there on his newly-bought farm. He would learn. He would fly.

So he finally managed to dig up a few dozen acres, way the hell and gone up an inlet that someone had blessed with a long unpronounceable Indian name. "Find the asshole of Nowhere and go ten miles up it!" was all the directions the half-drunk real-estate agent had condescended to supply. As soon as he found the place, Walleye started in clearing the land for his farm. Inspired, he worked like a man possessed, digging and filling and chopping and gouging, slapping up fences and hacking down trees. Before long, the fields rose out of the tangles of scrub-brush, naked and furrowed, as if they'd been waiting there, camouflaged by trees. The first year a farmhouse appeared in a clearing; the next there were stables and silos and barns. Soon there were buildings all over the hillsides, then orchards with fruit trees and meadows full of cattle, then duck ponds and trout streams, then trestles and turrets and bridges and towers. By the time Walleye calmed down and recovered from this strange bout of madness, he had very nearly covered every square foot of ground he owned and was frantically buying up gullies and rock bluffs and God knows what else from the suddenly money-mad locals. Then one day the whole business passed from his mind like a tedious, labyrinthine dream. His head cleared and there he was, up to his ass in the foul-smelling mudflats that bordered the inlet. He regarded the long-handled sledge-hammer he was holding up over his shoulder as if it had suddenly grown there. What the fuck am I doing? he wondered. A long line of tar-blackened timbers, which he had apparently pounded into the muck of the mudflats, ranged out all around him, a mute, inexplicable sign. It was already nightfall. It was pissing down rain. A stray cow was stuck in the goulash behind him, struggling and mooing forlornly. He had no sooner drawn back the hammer to kill it, than he noticed the girl on the shore.

She was sitting on the slope that ran down from the farm to the inlet, surrounded by sea grass and dried clumps of fern. She was skinny and her blonde hair hung lank to her shoulders. Her wrist bones were fragile and her neck thin and long. She looked up at Walleye, her eyes wide and frightened, and started to warble and chirp like a bird.

Whoever she was, she became Walleye's wife. Annalee, as he called her, was almost a mute. *Almost*, that is, in that while she could no more speak the King's English (or any other language, for that matter) than a pig could dance polkas, she could sure as hell whistle and sing. Well, not *sing*, exactly: it was more of a sort of fluting noise she made, throaty and distant as wind in the alders, quiet as spring water rising through stone. Walleye gradually got used to this constant commotion, although sometimes he'd jump when she'd let loose a sudden bright jangle of bird song, brassy as church-bells, which she did every time she saw him approach.

Their lives settled down to a humdrum routine. Their chores and their projects. Their joys and their sorrows. The sun and the snow and the wheel of the seasons. The wind and the stars and the thin piss of rain on the dreary Pacific. The days and nights clicking on and off like a blind eye opening, closing. Time hung like fog in the eaves and the branches, drifting occasionally this way or that, from time to time clearing enough to reveal a little of a dull grey day, always the same day, with Annalee walking about in it, clucking and tossing her handfuls of grain to the bevies of chickens, who also clucked, or parting enough to show Walleye, dishevelled and pensive, hunched by the bench of his cluttered-up work-shop, carefully baring the bones in the wing of a freshly-trapped heron, its spindly neck draped on his wrist like a lily as he pared off its flesh with the rust-covered scalpel that was all that remained of the days of his youth. Supported by the monthly cheques that were still sent out from England each month and that found their way somehow, through some miracle fashioned of steamtrains and mailboats, all the way up to their home on the inlet, Walleye and Annalee settled in to married life. Slowly the years scuttled past them.

Then, one bright summer morning, they discovered that there was a catch to this situation. There Walleye was, standing at the edge of the inlet and watching as the seagulls went soaring out over the waves and the mudflats, when a little green mailboat came chugging and wheezing along up the inlet, a portentous occurrence indeed, as it wasn't the right time of month for their cheque. After what seemed like forever the boat scraped ashore on the clam shells and gumbo not ten feet away from where Walleye was standing, and a tiny man, shrouded in oilskins and sweating profusely, emerged from the wheelhouse and clambered ashore.

"You Jackson?" he spluttered, staggering under the weight of a huge khaki mailbag and peering at Walleye through grimy pince-nez.

Receiving no answer, he rummaged around in the depths of his satchel and finally fished out a damp scrap of paper with intricate creases and smudges of grease.

"This here's for you," he said, inching the strap of the mailbag down his shoulder and scratching a raw patch of flesh on his neck.

Dazed, Walleye stared at the telegram. ELIZABETH JACKSON DECEASED OFFSPRING ARRIVING DOMINION DAY TEN THIRTY TRAIN was all that it said on the sheet.

"What the Christ does it *mean?*" he moaned to the waves and the gulls and the wind as he crumpled the paper and tossed it away. The bearer of this mysterious message, however, had already scampered away down the shoreline, trailing a white swath of letters and postcards that gleamed on the sand and the rocks and the mudflats until they were caught up and wafted away. Reaching his tugboat, the little man pitched himself headfirst onto the stern deck and, having gained the wheelhouse, manoeuvred the roaring and clattering craft out to sea.

"I only deliver the fucking things, Mister," he shrieked from the midst of the black cloud of smoke that was billowing out of a ruptured exhaust pipe and almost obscuring the vanishing tug. "I ain't paid to fucking explain them."

Walleye sensed from the first that his luck had run out. He watched as the boat disappeared in the distance, the long furrowed scar of its wake healing over and leaving the clear waters glassy and calm. It was almost as if there had never been anyone there. No mailboats; no strange little men wearing oilskins; and above all no goddamn unsettling telegrams dropping like bombs from the clearest of skies to unnerve him. While he couldn't imagine what whoever had sent him that telegram wanted, he was sure that it could only be trouble. Not that the whole thing was absolute gibberish. The only name mentioned, Elizabeth Jackson, was more than familiar. Little Sour-faced Lizzie, as Walleye had called her, had been married to a shirt-tail relative of his, an impotent quivering wisp of a twice-removed cousin who'd died shortly after of a wasting disease. DECEASED, the message had stated. So much for Little Sour-faced Lizzie. But OFF-SPRING ARRIVING? What the devil did that mean? Had Lizzie presented the world with a brood of unlovable brats before dying? And were they now coming out here to sponge off him? Now there, Walleye decided, was a truly horrible thought. The wise thing to do, he reasoned, was to pretend that the telegram had been lost on its way out to Canada and had never arrived at the inlet. But then what if his family should cut off his cheques?

So there Walleye was early Dominion Day morning, having journeyed all night to get south to the railhead, all decked out and spruce as a corpse in its coffin, with his ancient black suit and his battered old top hat, his grey beard combed out in a stiff bristling fan on his stained cardboard shirt front and his eyeglasses tied to his head with a shoelace, awaiting the ten-thirty train from the east. In the fullness of time, it pulled up at the platform, engulfing poor Walleye in a thick cloud of steam.

Two small figures formed in the mist as it cleared. The smaller of these was a squat pig-eyed schoolboy, his round belly bursting from an ill-fitting blazer and his corpulent abdomen tightly encased in a long pair of grey flannel shorts. To his left his companion, a thin girl of fifteen or sixteen, was fussing about with a couple of carpetbags, looking for someone to pack them away for her. She was wearing a blazer and long woolly stockings, a huge pair of oxfords and a long pleated skirt. On her head was a wide straw boater, its pale violet ribbon adrift in the tangles of hair that uncoiled on her shoulders and flowed down her back. Noticing Walleye, she marched up and plonked down her bags at his feet.

"Are you, sir, by any chance our second cousin twice-removed?" she asked, picking a balled-up lace hanky from the sleeve of her blazer and violently blowing her nose. "By marriage, I mean, not by blood."

This much affirmed, she beckoned the little boy over and, daubing her eyes with the edge of her hanky, proceeded to look Walleye up and down critically, pausing occasionally to shake her head in disbelief or to utter an absurdly theatrical sigh.

"Well, I suppose we'd better be getting on then, hadn't we, Cousin?" she said. She carefully fingered the handkerchief back up her sleeve and, clearing her throat, nudged both the bags toward Walleye.

"You may address me, by the way, as Miss Hilary, or, if you prefer, as Miss Jackson," she continued, averting her eyes with a sour look and offering Walleye one limp, ringless hand to be kissed. Walleye regarded her well-bitten fingernails, muttering under his breath.

"This creature," the girl went on, waving in the direction of the fat little boy, "is my loathsome and utterly cretinous sibling. Tipton, I believe, is its name."

"Tip, not Tipton, you witch!" her brother snarled, aiming a kick at her ankles.

"Little pig," she said, smiling.

All things considered, the children settled in rather well to their new life in Walleye's home on the inlet. They adapted so quickly, in fact, that Walleye was shocked by their sudden metamorphosis. As though touched by the wand of a conjurer, both of them instantly sprouted a costume of gumboots and long baggy trousers and green-and-red plaid shirts with rumpled-up collars and huge lumpy sweaters emblazoned with eagles and odd-looking bears. Nor did it take them long to become acquainted with their neighbours, who in Walleye's opinion were nothing much more than a disreputable gaggle of no-account loggers with browbeaten women and scroungy-looking children: people whom he had always avoided. Walleye watched with mounting apprehension as

Tipton and Hilary shuttled back and forth through the bush to the loggers' shacks sprinkled on the hills above the inlet. God help us all, he thought, if they start bringing that crew around. Which, as it turned out, was exactly what they did.

In a matter of weeks, Walleye found himself drowning in a flood tide of mooches and loudmouths and drunks. Wolfpacks of dirty-faced, snivelling infants surrounded him constantly as he skulked from his house to his barn to his workshops, shrieking in his ears and calling him "Birdman," tugging at his pant-legs and yanking his beard. Annalee, for her part, spent most of her mornings untangling children from the old bits of rusted machinery Walleye had scattered all over the hayfields. The whole business upset her terribly. For years she had been queen of an insular kingdom, her life running as smoothly as a stream in a valley, centred on nothing but bird song and Walleye: now everything seemed to be falling apart. It seemed to her, at times, as if they must have offended some dark brooding power that lurked in the wilds, inhabiting all things that grew or were born there, simply by carving a piece from the forests around them to live on and order and claim as their own. Now it was all coming up through the floorboards: that darkness, that madness, that force beyond thought. It was there in the blank, mindless gaze of the evil-tongued gossips who leaned on the gateposts and questioned each move that she made as she made it. It was there in the snotty-nosed, insolent kids she was constantly shooing from under the tables, in the shrewd, smiling women who came round to offer their help while they filched what they could from her pantry and her larder, in the gaunt, mangy dogs who could somehow worm clear through the chicken-wire fences and harry the poor birds right out of their coops, in the crows that sat rasping outside in the branches, in the thistles and devil's club sprouting up out of the muck in her gardens, in the wind that brought rain, rain, and more rain forever and ever, no matter what hour and no matter what season, as if it were trying to put out a fire. It was hiding in all things and everyone out there, this dark god that gloried in chaos, in infinite growth. Slowly it narrowed the boundaries around her, driving her out of the light and the elements, deeper and deeper inside of herself. She finally shut herself up in her room like an invalid, cowering in her bed among a mountain of pillows, cooing forlornly and braiding her hair.

In her absence young Hilary lost no time whatever in taking things over and setting herself up as the lady of the house. Having once got her oar in, she began to remake the entire estate in her own image. For a kickoff, she quickly disposed of the few sticks of ratty old furniture Walleye had bought at a government auction and scattered at random all over the house. The next thing she chucked out was Walleye himself. Banished outside to a cot in his workshop, practically cut off from contact with Annalee, deprived of his rights in the home he'd created, Walleye muttered and fumed in the gloom of that shed. Menaced by landslides of bird bones and feathers, prey to the terrors of cold and starvation, an outcast adrift in a cruel world inhabited only by dumb barnyard creatures and garrulous, whiskey-soaked neighbours, he watched in despair as affairs in his mansion went rapidly downhill and straight to the dogs. As if the unwanted arrival of his godless, unwashed and unspeakable neighbours (not to mention their coarse broods of rustic delinquents) hadn't been more than enough to drive any sane man to the brink of distraction, a merciless fate smote him further when Hilary made friends with the dregs of the washed-up colonial gentry. Drawn by the news that a tender young lady of English extraction was bravely attempting to manage such a huge, rambling mansion, and sensing a rare chance to shake loose an acre or two of already-cleared farmland by simply appealing to her patriotic zeal, they descended on the inlet like a Biblical plague. In no time the house was a morass of Anglophile leeches, ratchet-jawed loafers who seemed to come slithering out of the cracks in the plaster, all tweed coats and plus fours and twitching moustaches, men without income or known occupation, whole families who seemed to have been bodily thrown to the edge of the Empire as if by some sort of centrifugal action that had dragged them away from the world they'd been born to without having had time to so much as change clothes or shave off their whiskers, people who seemed to have no more to do with the country around them than centaurs or aardvarks or hairy-assed wombats, men who would buttonhole Christ if he rose up among them and regale him with stories of how they'd have re-fought the seige of Khartoum.

The final blow, however, came with the arrival of yet another unexpected and unwanted guest. One morning a beat-up old truck pulled into the barnyard and a wizened little dwarf of a woman, no taller than a six-year-old child, hopped down from the driver's seat. She was smaller than anyone Walleye had ever seen before, and looked for all the world like some species of tropical bird with her tatters of satin and velvet for plumage and a stiff crown of red hennaed hair standing straight up like feathers from the top of her head. She was, as it turned out, a self-proclaimed witch who'd been passing herself off as a full-blooded Cree for so many years that she'd long since forgotten she wasn't, in spite of the fact that she spoke with a thick Irish brogue. A down-at-the-heels entertainer, she'd been touring the backwoods for years with her magic act, eking out an extremely precarious living, sleeping in the back of that old Fargo truck, the legend on the sides of which proclaimed in faded gilt letters her name and alleged occupation: LITTLE PRINCESS RAVENFEATHER: MEDIUM, SORCERESS, MAGE, AND CHANTEUSE. To Walleye's alarm and incomprehension, she announced her intention of moving into his mansion. The vibrations, she asserted, were absolutely perfect for the working of magic. She and Hilary were soon thick as thieves.

Baffled and frustrated, balked at every turn, Walleye threw himself into his work with a passion and singleness of purpose that was frightening to behold. Nailing the door of his workshop shut tight against further intrusions and only crawling out through the window once every night to forage for food, he began to sort methodically through the seemingly-infinite number of half-baked ideas he'd evolved through the years he'd spent in pursuit of his dream. A bird priest, an adept (his mind throwing sparks through that shadowy workshop), he hunched like a monk at his bench day and night. Building with tubing and bent bits of haywire, allowing for updraughts and downdraughts and doldrums, computing the angles of starlight and earthshine, dreaming of Tycho and Ursus and Kepler, of sky gods with hooked beaks and silvery talons, of Chaldeans perched on the steps of their ziggurats, of seraphs ascending the fires of the zodiac, of harpies and hawks and armillary spheres, he slowly, devoutly, precisely constructed the ultimate engine through which he could finally realize his purpose, his god-given, priestly vocation of climbing and wheeling and soaring away from the death-haunted grip of this slow-turning, ponderous planet, a chrysalis breaking the husk of its earthly cocoon and emerging, a Sphinx moth triumphant, free of the fetters of logic and reason, rising majestically upward to heaven on fragile, invincible wings. In the dark, fetid womb of his cavernous workshop it gradually, painfully came into being: a beautiful, terrible creature suspended on wires from a hook in the ceiling, alive to the least breath of air from the window, its steel rods and brass fittings gleaming and winking, an angular spider at rest in its web. There were four separate levels of long slanting bird wings, a tail like a rudder and fins bearing feathers, connected by tendons of thin copper wire. There were bicycle wheels hanging down from its belly, along with a harness to hold up its pilot and a chain-drive and pedals to power it aloft. Sundry things dangled on wires from the harness: a sextant, a spyglass, a compass, a lamp.

All that remained was to locate a pilot to take it up for a test flight, so that Walleye could observe how it flew from the safety of the barnyard (and so that he could blame it on the pilot if the whole thing collapsed in a tangle of feathers and plummetted into the salt chuck). The unanimous reticence displayed by the fortunate souls who were offered this singular honour, however, left Walleye right back where he'd started. Then one rainy morning the solution to his problems appeared, albeit in a strikingly unlikely form.

There Walleye was, flat on his back on the floor of his workshop, half-heartedly applying a fresh coat of wax to the already-glistening spokes of the starboard sidewheel of his flying machine, when who should come waddling straight through the door but his overfed ass of a cousin, little Tipton from over the seas. Ever a prominent figure on his elder sister's shit-list, it seemed he had also been banished from the house. Possibly overcome with paternal affection, Walleye leapt up and kicked the boy square in the ass. This gesture, combined with a fatherly cuff round the earhole, convinced the young fellow in no time at all that his destiny lay in the new field of flight. Strapped in the harness and perched on the pilot's seat, stubby legs manfully pumping the pedals, everything creaking and flapping around him, barely held back by the wires from the ceiling, young Tipton hovered and lurched in the murk of that workshop, a bulbous amphibian caught between elements, that infernal machine with its long streamlined wings taking over the use of his arms and his legs and his lungs and his bloodstream, consuming him utterly, making him part of its abstract, inhuman, unthinkable function, a sleek pterodactyl devouring its prey.

Soon all was in readiness. Walleye could hardly contain himself. After years of frustration and fruitless invention, everything seemed to be falling into place. Even at rest, the machine itself seemed to be straining at its moorings, and despite his rotundity Tipton turned out to be a natural pilot. Transformed by countless hours spent thrashing around in the grip of that contraption, if not by his cousin's unceasing harangues on the subject, the youngster developed an obsession with flying, a desire to life himself clear of the earth and its workings, that rivalled that of Walleye himself.

Then, on the very day Walleye had picked for his test flight, his whole fragile world flew apart.

It began with an ominous silence. As Walleye, bleary-eyed and weary, peered out the door of his workshop first thing in the morning, he was stunned by the calmness, the sheer unnerving serenity, the absolute absence of noises and voices, the emptiness ever expanding around him in clear waves and translucent, hollow-boned echoes, an ocean of no-sound that drowned out the world. Where had everyone gone? No faces appeared in the windows and doorways. Not a soul could be seen on the sidewalks and porches. Not a child sallied forth from the jungles of crabgrass. Even the sandpiles were barren of brats.

Anxious to get to the heart of the mystery, Walleye trudged up the path to his house. The stillness around him was awesome, unnatural. Not a damned thing was moving, wherever he looked. The pigsties were pigless, the stables deserted, the chicken coops moonscapes of feathers and chicken shit; the sky had even been scoured clean of birds. Then, just as Walleye arrived at the door of his mansion, the first sounds he'd heard in what seemed like forever came creaking and wheezing up out of the workshop as Tipton, unaware that the world all around him was now a wasteland, dutifully worked out on the flying machine.

Braced by the sound of another survivor, Walleye opened the door of his house and walked inside. When he saw what was left of his dining-room and parlour, he didn't know whether to shit or go blind. There was mud on the ceiling and the drapes were encrusted with cobwebs. The chairs and the tables were burned black or broken. The hallways and stairs were a river of ashes. There were footprints embedded in un-likely places, like fossils embalmed in primordial slime. On the ruins of the staircase, an elderly, vexed-looking lady sat, muttering softly and staring into space. She was holding the stalk of a frazzled umbrella, a lop-sided halo of charred, twisted spokes jutting out in a ring around the top of her head.

"Witchcraft!" she murmured. As Walleye approached her, she turned into air.

Avoiding the spot on the staircase where this ancient, unsettling vision had been sitting, Walleye made his way upstairs. There was no doubt in his mind who was responsible for wreaking this destruction on the world he had created; it had to be Cousin Hilary and her sorceress companion, Little Princess Who's-it. Before he tracked the pair of them down, however, he wanted to check on Annalee, who had been holed up in her bedroom and whom he hadn't seen in months. When he had finally succeeded in wading through the piles of debris on the staircase, he ran to the door of the bedroom and forced his way inside.

The canopied bed in which he and Annalee had slept was covered with cobwebs and its blankets were furred with dust. In the midst of a mountain of bolsters and patchwork quilts a small head was perched on two dust-covered pillows. A dry, reedy breath rose and fell through the dust. Horrified, Walleye crept nearer. He reached out and gingerly touched the parched lips of the occupant of the bed with just the tips of his fingers. He could hardly believe it was Annalee. It couldn't have been more than a few months since he'd last seen her, but she looked as if she'd been lying in that bed since the dawn of Creation. She had withered up to nothing and her face was lined with wrinkles. Her long hair was fanned out on the blankets all around her, interwoven with ribbons and feathers and bird bones, an intricate network of stiff yellow braids. The bedroom itself looked like a stateroom on the *Titanic*; the plaster had rained down in flakes from the ceiling, limp flaps of paper hung down from the walls. Even the light in the room looked decrepit; a pale tarnished silver, it languished in pools on the carpets and quilts.

The next thing Walleye knew he was back in the barnyard. For a moment he danced around rubbing his eyes and trying to cough up the dust of millennia. When he came to his senses, the first thought he had was to hunt down that skinny-assed prig of a cousin of his, put a couple of half-dollar stamps on her forehead, and mail her straight back where she'd come from. But where the hell was she? he wondered. Come to that, where was everyone else? He glared at the weathered grey walls of his buildings, all of which calmly stood there and glared back at him, mutely protesting their innocence.

23

And then, as the core of the dark, brooding silence broke open, a many-tongued creaking rose up all around him, a wheezing and flapping and buzzing and shrieking, a noise like an army of ill-tempered birds. Walleye froze to the spot on which he was standing and stared in amazement at the ground at his feet. Beneath him an ominous-looking shadow was growing; two huge wings reached out from his trembling shoulders, growing steadily longer and wider and darker as that god-awful racket became louder and louder until it echoed off every wall in the farmyard, a clanking as angry as the hammers of hell.

Walleye fell to his knees in the cowshit and gumbo of the barnyard. What the devil was happening? he wondered. Had he finally been transformed? Was his prayer being answered? He thought of the years he'd spent chasing a phantom, a winged man that hovered and soared in his visions, a mythical creature that was unfolding from deep inside him, searing his flesh with the light of its birth. Metamorphosed from a mere creature of the earth into a birdman, reborn from the fire of his dreams like the Phoenix, he leapt to his feet and capered around in the barnyard, flapping his long skinny arms like a fool.

Then the shadow that had been growing at his feet swam away from him and climbed up the side of his rain-weathered mansion, in the upstairs window of which Hilary and Little Princess Ravenfeather stood laughing and sticking their tongues out at Walleye. Walleye looked up just in time to see the winged shadow vanish from the wall of the mansion as Tipton, strapped to the harness of the flying machine, soared gracefully over the rooftop. God only knows how the boy had become airborne, but there he was flapping off into the distance, rising in a loose, lazy spiral above the treetops, then soaring out over the inlet and gradually disappearing into the haze above the sea.

Dazed at the loss of his moment of glory, deprived of the sea change he thought he'd accomplished, watching his hopes boil away into nothing, Walleye ran down the long muddy slope to the inlet, shaking his fist at the rapidly-vanishing form of his flying machine. Screaming abuse at the heavens above him, he waded out up to his waist in the waters of the inlet, pursuing the shadow that was receding before him, the ghost bird he'd been following forever and ever, a little man chasing a dream made of matchsticks, alone in the dark at the edge of the world.

"Come back here, you wing-thieving bastard!" he bellowed. "You weasel-assed son of a Christ-bitten Anglican whore!"

A Portrait of Helena Leafly, With Bees

If anyone had asked him what life was all about, Jake Leafly would have told them, without a moment's hesitation, that life was a pattern, an intricate design. It wasn't the things you ran into in this crazy world that mattered, he would probably have added: It was the way things fell together, and the way they fell apart.

Take bees, for example. Look at them one at a time, and you wouldn't think that they were good for much of anything. All they ever seemed to do with themselves, after all, was to fly around buzzing their brains out. But get yourself a couple of dozen hives full of the little buggers, and put them out in a meadow full of fireweed and blossoming clover, and you had yourself a machine for making honey.

It was as if each of the bees were a thread in some vast Persian carpet, like the ones that they sold at that hippie import shop in the Harbourside Mall in Nanaimo, so that you had to see a whole swarm of them working together before the pattern would emerge.

Which was something that Jake Leafly could do any time he liked.

Jake and his wife, Helena, had been keeping bees for twenty-five years, and there wasn't a little corner store from Port Alberni to Victoria that didn't have a jar or two of LEAFLY'S GOLDEN HONEY prominently displayed on its shelves. Tourists would drive fifteen or twenty miles down from the Island highway, just to stop in at their farm and buy a crock or two of their honey in bulk. A fancy health-food magazine that was published in Toronto had mentioned LEAFLY'S GOLDEN in its *Gourmand Of The Backwoods* column. It was a wonder, when you thought of it, that Jake Leafly wasn't rich.

26

Not that Jake himself ever gave a second thought to making money. Keeping bees, as far as he was concerned, was more of a religion than a business. It was his wife who had to worry about keeping things afloat.

And Helena Leafly had no head for business. The most fundamental principles of day-to-day commerce had always been impenetrable mysteries to her. It wasn't simply that she didn't *like* keeping the accounts or adding up figures: she seemed to have a physical aversion to mathematics. As a schoolgirl, she would creep into her Math class like some lost soul descending into the flames of the inferno, gasping like a beached fish and bugging her eyes out, in terror lest the teacher ask her to attempt some long division. Adding up her change in a supermarket was enough to give her three days of brain-numbing migraines. The mere thought of balancing the books made her nauseous.

God only knows how the business kept going. Every week or so, Helena would tie a cardboard box full of quart jars of honey onto the bockety roofrack of her faithful old VW beetle and make the rounds of all the corner stores up and down the Island, leaving the honey to be sold on consignment. The receipts she was given by the owners of these stores would invariably disappear into the voluminous pockets of her tatty old tartan jacket, where they would remain until they decomposed into fuzzy balls of lint.

If it weren't for the fact that the majority of the shopkeepers with whom the Leaflys did business were honest folk who paid up their accounts without having to be prompted, in all probability Jake and Helena would have starved. As it was, there was always a trickle of money coming in from one of their retailers or another, but they were never quite sure just how much they should be making, or where it should be coming from, or when it would arrive.

Under normal circumstances, the precariousness of their income caused the Leaflys surprisingly little worry. Their requirements, after all, were modest to say the least. Jake could rarely stomach anything except Shredded Wheat and honey, while Helena lived on cigarettes, washed down with cups of tea. Neither of them had bought a stitch of clothing since before they were married: old shoes could be sent to the cobbler; old clothes could be mended and patched. And as for entertainment, there was never any problem. Jake rarely did anything of an evening but stand at the window and stare at his beehives, and Helena's weakness for lurid romances could be indulged inexpensively at the Thrift Shop in town.

It was only when they needed a buck or two for something special, like an unforseen tax bill or a new set of brakes for the VW, that their lack of a steady income became a cause for concern. On these occasions, Helena would toss a case or two of honey into the back seat of the VW and beetle on in to the nearest hotel. Just by lugging the honey into the hotel beer parlour a jar at a time, she had discovered, she could pocket a day's wages in no time at all. It was amazing what a few beer would do to a man's sales resistance. There were men she'd known since childhood, Helena would tell you, card-carrying tightwads who'd skin a flea to save a penny, who would practically knock her over in their haste to buy her honey if she was lucky enough to catch them when they were properly in their cups.

That was the only thing that Helena had learned about doing business: Find yourself a fellow with a beer or two in his belly, and he'll buy the Graff Zeppelin and tow the damn thing home. In all of the years she'd been making the rounds of the pubs around Nanaimo, selling quart jars of LEAFLY'S GOLDEN to the pie-eyed and the plastered, she had only met one genuine exception to this rule.

Bud Posner could have drunk every last drop of beer in the world and stayed sober. Draft beer just ran right through him; he was immune to its effects. He would sit there by himself in the corner of the pub and just pour down one glass of cold draft after another from noon until midnight every day except Sunday, and never bat an eyelash or slur a single word. Helena had long since given up trying to sell her honey to Bud Posner: in all the years she'd known him, he had never bought a solitary atom of the stuff.

It wasn't LEAFLY'S GOLDEN or any other kind of sweet, sickening bee-juice that he wanted, Bud Posner would tell her, pausing briefly to drain another glass or two of beer between phrases; it was the benefit of her wisdom. What he wanted was advice.

Which was nothing out of the ordinary, as far as Helena was concerned. People were always asking her to tell them the meaning of life. Hardly a day would go by without someone or other—Chin Lee the grocer or fat Betty Walmsley or the woman with the blue hair who sat next to her at the Kiwanis bingo or the kid who pumped gas at the garage up on the highway, sidling up to her with a browbeaten, hangdog expression and whining,

"What's life all about, Mrs. Leafly? What the heck are we doing in this crazy old world?"

Now that was just the sort of nonsensical question that her husband would have relished, Helena would often think, when confronted with these querulous neighbours. Ask Jake what he thought about the Meaning of Existence, and he'd stand there jabbering about how everything was a pattern until the sun had burned out like a 40-watt lightbulb and the earth had been sold for scrap to some little green man from Mars.

Him and his goddamn *patterns*: It made you dizzy just to listen to him, mumbling on and on about how the universe was made up of a network of complex patterns, each one of which was just a small part of some other, larger pattern, so that the pattern of the particles revolving in an atom and the pattern of all the stars in all the galaxies in all Creation were really, if you examined them, the very same thing on a different scale. It was all, he would bluster, waving his long, bony fingers at the ceiling as if he were attempting to pull together the threads of his tenuous theory, exactly like the patterns in a swarming hive of bees.

Helena had been listening to Jake's lame-brained theories

about patterns for so long that it was starting to make her seasick just to look at a patterned carpet. She couldn't even visit her friend Wildflower McCloskey, who ran the *Mandalay Treasure Trove* shop in the mall in Nanaimo, without feeling that the huge Persian carpets that covered the Treasure Trove's walls, floor and ceiling were about to dissolve into a swarm of buzzing insects. It was a menace to her sanity, having to spend her life with Jake.

Not that Helena couldn't have told you a thing or two about patterns herself, if she'd wanted to: there were times when she thought that her whole life was the working out of some devious pattern, as if she'd been put on this earth for the amusement of some bored, sadistic Fate.

Take her name, for example. Her maiden name was Palmer, and her father had been the minister at the little church in Lantzville, just up the highway from Nanaimo, and a man whose devotion to the theatre had far exceeded his devotion to God. As his wife had given birth while he was at the church hall performing *Faustus* with Ye Olde Lantzville Players, the local little theatre, it hadn't taken much imagination for him to hit on a Christian name for his newborn daughter. And Helena Palmer was a reasonable name for any girl, as Helena's mother was forced to admit. While conceding to her husband's choice in a first name for their daughter, however, the preacher's wife had stipulated that two middle names be added, names that had been in her family since Methuselah was a runny-nosed boy.

And so, burdened down with this excess baggage, Helena had been doomed to go through life as *Helena Eleanor Laurentian Palmer*. Or, if you reduced it to her initials, plain old H.E.L.P.

HELP!

It couldn't have been more appropriate if she had dreamed it up herself. All through her girlhood she had been plagued with a sense of impending disaster, as if the sky were about to come crashing down around her ears at any moment, or the earth to open up beneath her feet and let her fall right down to the centre of the world. While her contemporaries strided purposefully through life, bounding like so many antelopes from one triumph to another, Helena had always kept to herself, convinced that any action on her part would be an invitation to disaster, and that the only reasonable solution was to look for a safe place to hide. It was almost as if that name of hers had determined the course of her whole existence, as if the pattern of those four letters was the blueprint of her life.

It was hardly any wonder, then, that she was anxious to get married. It was the only way that she could think of to get rid of those accursed initials. When the neighbour's boy, Jake Leafly, proposed, she practically carried him into the church.

It wasn't until after the wedding was over, and they were standing around in her father's churchyard getting pelted with rice and confetti, that Helena realized she'd made a terrible mistake.

"Congratulations, Mrs. Helena Leafly!" one of the wedding guests shrieked, strafing Helena with another volley of confetti.

As Helena grinned back at the woman, it hit her. Her name, as a married woman, would be Helena Eleanor Laurentian Leafly. And her initials, heaven help her, would be H.E.L.L.

"Oh, *hell*!" she moaned, barely suppressing the urge to run screaming off into the distance, "out of the goddamn frying pan and into the goddamn fire."

Not that her life with Jake had been a hell-on-earth, exactly. It was more like a sort of limbo, a bee-infested purgatory in which every day was like every other, and every year the same year, so that they seemed to be existing in one endlessly-repeated moment, in a succession of days as identical as the cells in an infinite hive. Jake, in his simplicity, saw the whole thing as a marvel, and wandered through life lost in awe at the symphony of shifting shapes and forms that was unfolding all around him, but Helena saw the days of her life as the bars of a cage that contained her, a web of predestination from which no living thing could escape. There were times when she was so unspeakably bored that she could *feel* herself growing older, sitting there puffing a roll-your-own at the tatty kitchen table while her husband clumped through the clovered fields in his clumsy beekeeper's outfit, nodding sagely at the hives with his helmetted head like an astronaut walking on Saturn. There were times when she could have happily cut his throat, and left his carcass for his everlasting bees.

Not that there was much chance of her actually up and murdering her husband. What difference would it make to her life, after all? If she wasn't stuck out on a honey farm with a bee-crazy old duffer who thought he was Aristotle, she would only be mixed up in some even-worse disaster: it was her fate to be unhappy, and there was no escaping fate. The best that she could hope for was that Jake would go on living, because when he finally kicked the bucket she would probably wind up marrying Attila the Hun or Adolph Hitler and have to spend the rest of her life enslaving Asia or goose-stepping all over the lawn.

So instead of trying to change her life, Helena did her best to ignore it. How much longer could it go on for, after all? Another twenty years or so, and she'd be shut of the whole messy business, securely in her cosy grave, without a worry in the world.

In the meantime, however, she had plenty to keep her busy. While Jake looked after the fields and the hives and did the majority of the work collecting honey, she could always amuse herself washing out jars or sticking on the LEAFLY'S GOLDEN labels. And when she wasn't puttering around the place, or out making her endless deliveries, she could beetle on in to the Harbourside Mall and kill some time with Wildflower McCloskey, who was always glad to have someone to chew the fat with in her shop.

Wildflower had been some sort of hippie back in the 'sixties, and had drifted to the Island with so many others of her generation, in search of a Thoreauesque paradise among the pulp mills and the fog. After idling away a dozen years thrashing out folk songs on homemade dulcimers and choking down out-of-season oyster stew in a leaky geodesic dome in the backwoods, she had come to Nanaimo and gone into business selling Oriental gee-gaws and books on meditation —at exactly the same time that everyone else in the world had said to hell with the Age of Aquarius and gone into real estate or peddling insurance. Undaunted by the obvious fact that everything she had in the store was at least ten years out of fashion, she sat there resolutely among the silver-plated roach-clips and the Jimi Hendrix posters, gazing in stupified wonder at the polyestered salesmen and spikey-haired adolescents of the uncongenial 'eighties, who rarely even *saw* her store as they sauntered through the mall.

It was hardly any wonder, then, that she looked forward to Helena's visits. And besides, there was something so natural, so downright *organic* about old Mrs. Leafly. She would wander in from the shopping mall in her threadbare tartan jacket, peering shyly at Wildflower through her stringy fringe of grey-white hair that looked as if a blind man had cut it with tin-snips, her scrawny hands clutching the quart jar of LEAFLY'S GOLDEN that she inevitably brought along as a present. Then she'd plonk herself down among the lava lamps and the boxes of misshapen pottery, accept the cup of herbal tea that Wildflower inevitably offered, and sit there for hours without saying a word while her hostess babbled on endlessly about life on the Astral Level—which, judging by Wildflower's descriptions, was even more boring than life in the real world.

Helena, for her part, looked on her shopkeeper friend in just about the same way she looked on her husband. This Wildflower girl, with her Theda Bara wardrobe and her esoteric theories about parallel dimensions and her bearded friends who had given up good-paying jobs to shuck oysters on leaky old fishboats, seemed almost as eccentric as Jake.

But these days nearly everyone seemed to have some hare-brained theory about the Meaning of Existence. And it wasn't just the obvious flakes like Jake and Wildflower, either: there were plenty of perfectly respectable folks living right around Nanaimo, people whom Helena herself had known since they were snotty-nosed brats in grade school, who lived in fear of being blown to bits by UFOs from the planet Zargon, or who were waiting for the ghost of Elvis to rise up from his grave and redeem them, ushering in a billion years of peace and love on earth.

Sometimes Helena would drive for hours around the familiar streets of Nanaimo, gazing in absolute bafflement into the windows of nondescript houses, in each one of which, she felt certain, unimaginable lives were unfolding, desperate plans were hatched and irrevocable actions taken, whole families struggled like captured flies in sticky webs of predestination, made sacrifice to nameless gods and appeased imaginary demons, as they frantically tried to free themselves from the patterns of their lives.

It was while she was engaged in one of these endless cruises through the suburbs, weaving up and down the streets and craning her neck out the window, marvelling over the foolishness of humanity in general, that she caught sight of her old friend Bud Posner lying tits-up in the ditch. Posner, of course, was the last man on earth she'd have thought to find drunk in the gutter. While his adult life—and much of his childhood— had been one long attempt to get plastered, he had never, as far as Helena knew, met with anything resembling success. It was enough to break your heart, in fact, to see him sitting there in the corner of the beer parlour sober as a deacon, pouring down gallons of icy draft to no effect whatsoever. It was like watching someone try to hang-glide with an anchor in his pants.

But there was no doubt about it; it was definitely Posner. His awesome belly, the product of years of quaffing beer, protruded from the scurf of weeds in the ditch like a beehive in the centre of a meadow. His drunken snores buzzed loud enough to be audible above the blatt of her VW. He sounded like a swarm of bees on a windless summer evening, Helena thought, as she switched off the ignition and clambered out of her car. Scurrying across the street, she looked down at her friend in the ditch.

Was he *really* drunk? she wondered. Had he finally gotten plastered? One look at the beatific smile on his face as he lay there snoring like a poleaxed hippo was enough to remove any doubt from her mind. How wonderful he must feel, she thought, to have succeeded after all those years. Moses must have felt like that when he reached the Promised Land.

It was obvious, however, that she would have to take him home. God knows how he had found his way to this rather antiseptic suburb in the first place: it was miles from the hotel where he usually did his drinking, and even farther from the shack that he called home. Could she possibly pick him up and drag him over to the door of her VW? Assuming that she managed that Herculean feat, could she then cram him into the car? Impossible as it seemed, she would have to make an effort. She could hardly leave the poor man lying snockered in the ditch.

As she bent down to grasp Bud's beefy arm, a flicker of movement caught her eye—a golden spark that seemed to have emerged from the sleeve of Bud's sweater. It zipped past Helena's startled ear, buzzing like a runaway electron. She was halfway out of the ditch again before she realized what it was that she'd seen.

"Only a goddamn bee..." she muttered, sliding back down to Posner. "Goddamn things are everywhere you turn this time of year."

But before she could get to Bud again, another bee rose toward her. Then another and another, and the air was full of buzzing. In a moment Bud's whole body was a heaving swarm of insects. It levitated slowly from its bed among the crabgrass, shivered into beads of light, a web of graceful motion, and dispersed among the shrubs and trees along the shady street.

Helena stood flummoxed with one foot in the ditch for a moment, gazing up into the canopy of leaves above her with a

35

look of mute incomprehension. Then she dragged herself onto the road again and wobbled across to her VW.

It was that idiot Jake and his patterns, she thought. He had finally driven her crazy. She would wind up making wallets in the Home for the Bewildered, just from listening to him babbling on and on about his theories. From now on everything she looked at would probably dissolve into so many atoms. She'd be walking around in a universe of buzzing, swarming bees.

Her VW, however, seemed solid enough, and the street that it sat on wasn't moving. Wedging herself behind the wheel, she cautiously turned on the engine. Oblivious to metaphysics, the VW thrummed into life. Reassured of her precarious sanity, Helena shifted the car into gear.

It was then that she heard the buzzing. It seemed to come from deep inside her, as if she had swallowed an electric blender. Looking down, she saw that the tip of one of her fingers seemed to be detaching itself from the knuckle. Leaving its perch on the gearshift, it flew up at her, buzzing obscenely. In a moment the rest of her hand had dissolved, and her whole body seemed to be pulsing.

Perhaps, as her molecules swarmed out the windows and vents, she indeed saw the world as a pattern. Or perhaps it was only madness, and what she saw was simply *her* world dissolving. In any case her bulbous car came to rest against a hydrant, its tiny engine buzzing like an angry swarm of bees.

*   *   *

While Helena was away that afternoon, Jake was hard at work gathering honey. The moment she left the house, he put on his beekeeper's outfit. Having donned the wide, bell-shaped hat with its long skirt of netting and insinuated his fingers into stiff leather gauntlets, he stumbled down the rickety stairs and clumped across the yard. Pausing for a moment in the spikey strands of couchgrass at the edge of the meadow, he contemplated the emerald field with its neat rows of conical beehives, each one of which was a microcosm of the universe as a whole. Then, feeling less like a simple

36

farmer than the high priest of some primitive religion, he passed among the buzzing throngs like the Pope among his faithful, waving a benediction with his yellow plastic bucket and stooping occasionally to gather up the molten gold that was the tribute of his flock. Alone among his beehives, Jake felt charged with the power of nature, as if each of the hives were a dynamo and he the lone conductor. His nerve-ends seemed to crackle with a tingling electrical fire.

Normally, Jake would linger a few hours in the cool fields with his beehives, and then, having filled a bucket or two with fresh honey, reluctantly trudge back to the house before Helena came home. Just as he was about to pack up his buckets and head for the farmhouse, however, he slowly began to realize that there was something peculiar going on. There seemed to be fewer and fewer bees in each succeeding hive he came to, and their omnipresent buzzing seemed to be growing fainter with each passing moment. The horrifying thought that there might be something wrong with his precious insects sent Jake scurrying up and down the symmetrical rows of beehives in a panic. It wasn't until he thought to look up that the mystery was solved.

The whole swarm had gathered into a black knot that hovered, pulsating rhythmically, in the crystalline sunlight at the far end of the meadow. Bees swirled out of the long grass toward it like water drawn into a whirlpool. Its buzzing seemed somehow purposeful, charged with inscrutable intention. Jake had never seen anything like it in all of his years on that farm.

Tearing off his veiled hat and shielding his eyes against the dazzling sunlight, Jake peered at the dark, amorphous shape that hung above the meadow, muttering to itself in an unknown, unknowable language, like the mind of an alien god.

An then, as Jake stood there staring in his cumbersome bee-keeper's outfit, nervously clenching and unclenching his fists in their clumsy leather gauntlets, the swarm of bees sank slowly to the ground, then congealed and became coherent, forming itself into the mute, accusing figure of his wife.

A Rural Tale

Lemuel leapt down from the seat of his tractor and glared at the ground at his feet. If that isn't enough to frost a man's balls, he thought, kicking at the dry, dusty earth with the toe of his gumboot, I'm damn sure I don't know what is. Year after year you spend scratching around in the earth like some shit-for-brains chicken, and look what you get for it: uncooperative dirt!

Lemuel had been fighting a grim losing battle with soil, or the lack of it, for so long that now, even with those idiots in the government sending him pension cheques month after month and nothing to do for the rest of his life but to sit on his ass on the porch and get plastered, he simply couldn't bring himself to give up and quit. A man with a mission, he leapt out of bed before dawn every morning, shaved with one hand as he spooned down his watery gruel with the other, dressed as he sprinted outside to his tractor, threw slops to the hogs as he sped past the barnyard, and was already frantically hacking away at the recalcitrant ground with his pick by the time that his good-for-nothing rooster, Old Buck, reluctantly dragged himself up on a fencepost and gargled a few listless squawks at the sun.

But no matter how many hours he spent digging and ploughing, no matter how much manure he shovelled into the furrows, no matter how many harrows he blunted on bedrock, no matter how many creeks he diverted for irrigation, that land of his just couldn't—or *wouldn't*—grow crops.

It hadn't always been that way, of course. When Lemuel's grandfather had first carved that farm out of pure virgin forest, it had been the envy of all the other farmers on the coast. It was the closest thing to the Garden of Eden that you could possibly imagine, they said, with azure springs and citrus groves and miles of rolling meadows, and was so favoured by the climate that the clover bloomed in March.

Lemuel could still remember running barefoot through those meadows, a million billion years ago, when he was young and wild and free. In his grandfather's day that farm had been a place you could be proud of. If only, he lamented, it could be that way again.

One look at that dustbowl that he lived in, however, was enough to remind him of the futility of his dream. Every day of his life he had worked himself to a frazzle, and every day he'd wound up in absolute despair.

But this day, as it turned out, was somewhat different from the rest. As Lemuel stood cursing his fate in that bare field, a small puff of grey dust appeared in the distance, grew gradually higher and thicker and darker, acquired a chorus of deep-throated rumbles, and slowly took shape as it roared up the driveway: an ancient DeSoto with rust-pitted fenders that clattered and lurched to a stop in the yard. In a moment the door of the huge car creaked open and an old man, older even than Lemuel himself, pried himself cautiously out of the driver's seat and peered all around through the settling dust. He was as big as a barn door and as ugly as Satan: a ham-fisted troll with two burning blue eyes. With the sun at his back and his grizzled hair shining, he waddled a few awkward steps toward Lemuel, paused with his hand on his heart and moaned *Brother!*, then rolled his eyes heavenward panting and drooling, and fell with a smack on his face in the dust.

For a moment the world stood stock-still on its axis. The sun dimmed, the wind calmed, and everything shuddered. Horrified, Lemuel made his way over to the spot where the stranger was lying, an inert lump of matter in the centre of his farm. Turning the ancient hulk sunny-side-up, he gingerly scrapped the dust from its huge placid face with the toe of his gumboot, revealing the broad cheeks, the full lips, the network of wrinkles, the flat broken nose and the staring blue eyes of an elderly man who was no one on earth but his long-lost and little-missed brother, Elias by name, who had wandered away from that very same farm over forty years earlier, and who had not been seen since.

Elias had always been the family's black sheep. Even as a child, he had seemed to be boiling over with unspeakable lusts and unnatural ambitions. Trouble seemed to follow him around like a shadow. It was enough for him to sit on your porch for a few minutes for your life to be transformed into a litany of disasters. Your hens would stop laying. Your car would be stolen. Your house would burn down with your money inside it. Your sweet virgin daughter would give birth to triplets, each one of whom was blessed with two burning blue eyes. Before long, you'd be wandering around in a stupor on the highway, secure in the knowledge that sooner or later young Elias would come roaring along in someone else's car and run you over, ending your miseries once and for all.

Although only a few years younger than his demoniacal brother, Lemuel was everything that Elias was not. While Elias was garrulous, Lemuel kept to himself, preferring the company of shovels and hoes to the comfort of human companions. While Elias had ravished half the women in the province, and was not above leaping on the heifers in the barn if he couldn't find an even vaguely willing farmgirl, Lemuel was terrified of women, and would stammer like a schoolboy well into his forties at the mere thought of sleeping with a female. While Elias was a human volcanic eruption, a hydrogen bomb in the guise of a farmboy, poor old Lemuel was duller than ditch water. It was hardly surprising that Elias and he were never able to get along with each other. They were oil and water, so to speak, all their lives.

"Elias?" Lemuel whispered, as he knelt down to listen for breath at those thick lips beneath him. There was none. The old boy was dead.

*　　*　　*

It was almost dark by the time Lemuel finished burying his brother. As he climbed back on his tractor and chugged toward the farmhouse, he gazed in abject surrender at the dusty earth all around him, that Purgatory on which he had come to spend his life. His mind was full of memories of his childhood and his family; the evening wind was whispering with the voices of his past.

Once, almost sixty years ago, when he was a boy of twelve or thirteen, Lemuel's grandfather had told him the history of that farm.

He had—he'd said—arrived in Halifax, Nova Scotia on a clipper ship from Portsmouth, and set out to ride the CNR train all the way to the Pacific, where he'd heard that a man could make his fortune by panning for gold in the streams. Penniless, he couldn't afford the price of a ticket to British Columbia, and had been obliged to cross the country sitting on top of the train. It was while he was up there, clinging to the catwalk in the midst of a snowstorm somewhere in Manitoba, that Lemuel's grandfather had found God.

God, as it turned out, was a four-foot-tall Welshman with huge bushy eyebrows and hair as black as coal dust who lived on the roof of the CNR caboose.

"Hello?" Lemuel's grandfather had ventured, peering at the stranger through the haze of snow and the smoke from the locomotive.

"Hello yourself, Boyo!" the Welshman replied. He had made himself a sort of tent out of Hudson's Bay blankets and scraps of yellowed sailcloth, and was sitting cross-legged in front of a kerosene stove, stirring a pot of what looked like leek soup.

"And what might you be staring at, Sonny Jim?" he continued. "Have you never come face to face with your Creator before now?"

"Creator?"

"Well, that's who I am, see. Jehovah Allfuckingmighty. Good Welsh name, look you..."

Winking slyly at Lemuel's grandfather, the Welshman pulled a mickey of rye out of his waistcoat picket, gulped a copious mouthful, and smacked his lips with delight.

"As for yourself, Sonny Jim," he went on, "the best place

41

for you is out on Vancouver Island. Just like back home it is, full of coal mines and mountains. And the corn grows so fast you have to hire folk to eat it."

"But there's no gold on Vancouver Island," Lemuel's grandfather protested, hollering as loud as he could over the anguished yowl of the steam engine's whistle.

The train was about to plunge into a tunnel.

"All the gold in the world is in your mind, you silly bugger..." was all that Lemuel's grandfather heard of the Welshman's rebuttal. And then, like a thunderclap, "HEED THE WORD OF THE LORD!..."

When the train emerged from the tunnel, the little man had disappeared.

The only regret he had, Lemuel's grandfather used to tell him, was that he didn't take that crazy Welshman's advice a little sooner. Arriving in Vancouver, he had set out for the Klondike, still intent on finding his fortune in the bottom of a gold pan, and it wasn't until five years later that, having been robbed blind at least once by every tinhorn in the Yukon, he had found himself back in Vancouver and utterly penniless once again. Stealing a boat from the dock in Coal Harbour, he had headed for Nanaimo with the idea of getting a job in the coal mines, half-hoping that he might be lucky enough to drown along the way. Somewhere out in Georgia Strait, he must have fallen asleep at the tiller, as he woke up beached on a rocky shore with the bottom ripped right out of his boat.

There has to be a town around here somewhere, he decided. Clambering up the beach, he set off through the woods. By nightfall he was so lost he couldn't have found his ass with both hands and a searchlight: every tree on that island was the twin of every other, and every rock and bush he came to was the mirror-image of the one he'd just walked past. Giving up, he crawled into a hollow in the earth and covered himself with moss and branches, quite prepared to meet his Maker—even if it was for the second time.

Next morning, he was awakened by the rasping of a crow. Looking up, he saw a dark shape high above him in the branches. Crawling out of the hole where he'd been sleeping, he picked up a slab of rock and heaved it at the bird.

But instead of simply flapping away, or cawing abuse at him, as he might have expected, the crow stepped daintily off its branch and fluttered down toward him

where it flowed—
flowed, goddamn it—

into the body and the being of a beautiful young woman. Her skin was as brown as a berry and her eyes as clear as crystal. Her hair was long and black and hung in waves around her shoulders. When she spoke to Lemuel's grandfather, he could hear her voice right inside his head.

Whoever the woman was, she had come to stay with Lemuel's grandfather. Together they cut down trees and built a cabin in the middle of the forest. Together they cleared a patch of land and cultivated Indian corn and wild potatoes. With every passing day the patch of land became larger and more fertile. Springs rose out of solid rock and the sun shone brightly in the middle of winter. Lemuel's grandfather learned to love that place and the woman who had helped him build it.

And then one day she turned back into a crow and flew away.

Unable to understand how such a being could have existed, Lemuel's grandfather decided that he must have created her himself. However outlandish an idea this may have seemed, it turned out to be his salvation, as it led him to discover that he could dream things into being—He simply had to dream of things, and they would miraculously appear. At first, out of modesty, he would only dream small things: a bottle of good Scotch whiskey, a slim book of limericks, a shaving brush and razor, a box of Havana cigars. As time passed, however, he became increasingly ambitious. It wasn't long before that farm of his was one of the largest in the province, and his farmhouse looked like something out of a novel about the Confederate south.

43

And then, concerned about his own mortality or planning for the future, Lemuel's grandfather went to sleep one night and dreamed himself a son.

Which, as it turned out, was a terrible mistake. That son, who was Lemuel's father, was the ruination of their farm. His entire life was dedicated to screwing up everything Lemuel's grandfather had created. By the time he finally passed away, when Lemuel was thirty-five or forty, those lush rolling meadows had come to resemble the Kalahari desert, and the cattle were all so starved and inbred that you couldn't get an ounce of milk from a full-grown cow.

Now everyone will tell you that some folks just aren't cut out for farming, and that others find the work too hard or can't take the isolation. And everyone's heard stories about farmers who gamble away the seed money playing five-card stud with travelling salesmen, or who drink up all the profits before the crops are even planted; but it wasn't any of these common failings that made Lemuel's father such a godawful farmer. It was the word of the Lord that made him go and wreck that miraculous farm.

Lemuel's father was addicted to religion the way that some men are addicted to whiskey. And it wasn't any of your common-or-garden, watered-down Protestant, mamby-pamby, go-to-church-on-Sunday-and-do-what-the-hell-you-like-in-the-meantime stuff that interested him, either: it took 150-proof Bible-thumping, speaking-in-tongues-and-testifying, praise-the-Lord-and-damn-the-devil evangelical moonshine to quench his metaphysical thirst. While other boys stayed up all night reading sunbathing magazines under the blankets and caught hell from their parents for puffing cigarettes or sneaking drinks of their old man's hard cider, he passed his boyhood listening to fire-and-brimstone preachers on the wireless and memorizing passages on damnation from the Scriptures. Saturday night would find him in the main street of the neighbouring village, chained to the door of the dance hall with SATAN ENJOYS HIMSELF scrawled in red crayon on his forehead, while on Sundays he'd be writhing on the floor of some revivalist's tent in the backwoods, chewing the legs off the folding chairs and howling like a dog.

Obsessed with his salvation, Lemuel's father had no time for playing farmer. Besides, he would tell you, all that greenery was repulsive. If the Lord had wanted healthy crops and fields full of contented cattle, he'd have damn well put them on the planet himself, and there would never have been any need for all this nonsensical digging and ploughing. And there was something positively obscene about the sight of all those acres of lush vegetation: all that chlorophyll gushing around in every direction; all those moist, humid furrows lying there just dying to be seeded; all those germinated seedlings practically spurting up out of the earth. It was enough to give a God-fearing fundamentalist a case of the spiritual willies, the way that blaspheming farm insisted on bringing forth a bountiful harvest every year. Hadn't the Lord intended mortal existence to be an endless round of sorrow and lamenting? Wasn't every good Christian farmer supposed to spend his life cursing his fate and tearing his hair out in handfuls, while plagues of locusts devoured his crops, floodwaters washed his barn and silo down the river, his wife ran away with a card sharp from godless Toronto, and the whoopingcough carried off his first-born child? Well of course he was! What possible use would heaven be, after all, if life on earth was just as good?

In Lemuel's father's considered opinion, that farm was an affront to every Christian eye that beheld it. When the old man, Lemuel's grandfather, died, dreaming himself into nothingness one balmy August morning, his son lost no time whatever in putting things to rights. Not that turning that paradise-on-earth into a wasteland was easy. It took long years of backbreaking work before Lemuel's father could even begin to accomplish his God-given mission. Every atom of that farmland seemed to fight against his efforts, as if the soil itself were determined to grow tons of grain and produce. The weather was fiendishly warm every autumn, no matter how hard Lemuel's father prayed for an early frost to blight his orchards. You couldn't buy a single hailstone for all the money on the planet, and you'd have thought that every cutworm in the province had gone on strike.

Undaunted by the setbacks he suffered at the hands of a bountiful nature, Lemuel's father worked unceasingly in his righteous pursuit of failure. While other farmers lolled around selling foodstuffs and counting their profits, he was out in all weathers strewing rocks around the hayfields, grafting wild crabapple branches onto the pruned limbs of his fruit trees, diverting irrigation streams away from any usable farmland, filling in duckponds with the poor ducks still in them, and planting chickweed in the middle of the garden. Every evening he would lock the cows out of the barn, and every morning he'd play his accordion in the henhouse, in an attempt to put the chickens off their laying.

By the time that Elias and Lemuel had grown up, the farm was already a shambles. Soon after, their father decided that his good works were complete, and took a job at the rendering plant in the village, where he could spend each day covered in maggots and blood, happily tearing the hides off dead horses. Every evening he'd come stomping up the front steps of the farmhouse, peel off his grisly coveralls in the middle of the sagging verandah, and stride through the front door stark naked, picking stray maggots out of the hair on his forearms, as if he were Lazarus returning from the dead.

When his father finally perished, falling headlong down a cistern while strolling around the barnyard bellowing sermons at the livestock, Lemuel set out like a man possessed to restore that piece of farmland to its long-vanished former glory, to resurrect the paradise that his father had brought to ruin. It had taken half a lifetime for him to realize his folly. No farmer that was ever born could make a seed grow on that wasteland. It was as if there were something missing in the soil on that particular part of the planet, as if some vital force had been sucked right out of the earth and sent careening off into the distance, leaving nothing behind but a lifeless, useless, hopeless sea of dust.

It was across that arid ocean that Lemuel's tractor clanked that evening, delivering its driver to the front verandah of his farmhouse, over which he clumped in black despair to huddle in his bed.

* * *

When Lemuel woke up the next morning, he was sure that he had died in the night. He could hear angelic voices crooning somewhere in the yard beneath the window, accompanied by the yodels of his neighbour's Irish setters and the croupy shriek of Old Buck from his fencepost near the barn. Had the angels come to pack him off to the promised land? he wondered.

It was hardly a vision of paradise that greeted his eyes when he pulled back the curtains and peered out into the barnyard, however—unless, of course, God had sold the place to the Ringling Brothers Circus, or turned it into a holiday camp for the criminally insane. Parked in the middle of the yard was a schoolbus, or what had once been a schoolbus in a previous incarnation, and was now a sort of rolling shanty-town, a tenement on wheels. It had been sloshed with bright fluorescent paint from one end to the other, through which corroded patches bloomed like suppurating chancres. The fenders were rusted fine as lace, and the headlights stared off at odd angles. The roof had been shorn off at the tops of the windows and replaced with a shack made of rough cedar shingles, from which protruded weathervanes and rusty tin chimneys. Along one side in burning gold letters was painted the slogan: RESURRECTION EXPRESS.

It wasn't the ramshackle schoolbus that caught Lemuel's attention as he stared out his bedroom window that bright summer morning, however: it was the gang of strangers lolling around on the couchgrass that passed for a lawn. There must have been more than a dozen of them, counting the children. There were young men with shaved heads and long, flowing whiskers; plump girls with lank braids and loopy gold earrings; and ragtag kids rolling about like puppies in the dirt.

47

It was turning out to be quite a week, Lemuel decided: first his brother turns up and drops dead in the pasture, then a troop of wandering Bedouins materializes on the lawn. It was obviously time for him to start laying down the law. Grasping the crusty bib overalls that were hanging from the bedpost, he tugged them on over his nightshirt, yanked on his gumboots, fished his smiling teeth out of the glass on the bedside table, grabbed his 12-gauge from the cupboard and exploded out the door. He had no sooner crossed the verandah, however, than a curious transformation overcame the group of strangers. Every single one of them—men, women, and children—fell flat on his face with a smack in the dirt.

"The Lemuel!" they chanted, grovelling and rubbing their heads in the couchgrass. "At last we have found him! The Lemuel! The Lemuel!"

Eventually the nearest of them, a wild-eyed man with flowing robes and threads of grey in his stringy goatee, picked himself up and, gazing heavenward as if to thank his Creator for dreaming up couchgrass, took a hesitant step in the direction of the house.

"It is all just as Father Elias foretold it!" he whispered, gesturing expansively toward the swaybacked barn and the listing, cockeyed fences. "Here's the farmhouse where Father Elias was born. The barn where the heifers were transformed in maidens. The ashen fields where no seed has ever grown. The Lemuel standing guard like a watchdog. This is surely the Eden of which Elias has spoken! The hour of the Resurrection is surely at hand!"

"Father Elias!" the others sang, leaping up and capering about in the couchgrass. "At last we have found him!"

"Elias! Elias!"

"The Resurrection is at hand!"

It was late in the evening by the time Lemuel finally found out what his uninvited visitors were babbling about. By that time he'd invited them in and given them the run of the kitchen to make their dinner, which consisted of some sort of swampy-looking nettle stew. By nightfall his farmhouse, which was normally silent, seemed to sway with the tumult of voices, as the women sang folksongs while they scoured the pots and the men plucked out tunes on their banjoes. As the sky above the arid farm turned an ever-deeper amber, darkening to indigo along its eastern border, Lemuel dragged his rocking-chair out onto the porch and sat down. It was the first time in over thirty years that he hadn't worked himself into exhaustion, and the sensation of simply doing nothing felt more pleasant than he cared to admit. Before long, a few of the strangers came out to watch the sunset with him, and to tell him how they had run across his wandering older brother, and how they'd wound up being members of Elias' little tribe.

Elias, it seemed, had set himself up as a holy man back in the summer of '67. Roaming the country in a beat-up old bus, he had accumulated a veritable army of impressionable young disciples, each one of whom apparently regarded him as a sort of rustic Dali Lama, and supported him with generous gifts of their parents' hard-earned cash. While the "wisdom" that Elias had been dispensing sounded—to Lemuel at least—suspiciously like half-remembered phrases from their father's evangelical polemics, it had obviously been profound enough to satisfy his uncritical flock. In recent years, Elias had taken to telling stories about his childhood and his family, and his disciples had accepted these senile maunderings as their private Book of Revelations. When the time came, Elias had told them, he would journey back to his birthplace and fall dead into the arms of The Lemuel, his simple-minded brother who was the guardian of that farm. He would rise up again within forty-eight hours to be greeted by his faithful disciples, and then every seed and stalk of grass on that barren farm would blossom—but only for the scant few moments that it would take him to be reborn.

"Tomorrow he will rise at last!" a sallow girl with a ring in her nose hissed feverishly at Lemuel, fixing him with two sky-blue eyes as lifeless as lapis lazuli.

"Tomorrow!" the man with the goatee echoed, and all the disciples rose as one and trooped off to the bus and their beds.

That night, as he lay between the moth-eaten sheets on his hard narrow bed in that farmhouse, Lemuel found his thoughts returning to the story that Elias' followers had told him about the great event to come. Perhaps it was simply that he'd done nothing all day, or perhaps it was the unexpected excitement, but for some reason or other Lemuel found himself unable to fall asleep. For hours he tossed and turned on his bed, his fevered mind full of images of grass and trees and shining grain sprouting up from his arid pastures, of Elias leaping up from the dust of his grave with his hands full of germinated seeds. The disciples' tale was utter nonsense of course, Lemuel told himself as he lay there in the darkness— Who more than he knew how ludicrous it was to expect *anything* to rise up in that wasteland?—but no amount of logic would banish the prospect of lush rolling fields from his mind.

Toward dawn, Lemuel finally gave in to temptation and, pulling on his overalls, crept silently out the door. Tiptoeing past the ramshackle bus where his unwanted guests lay snoring, he made his way carefully out through the barnyard to the spot where he'd buried his brother in the field. There was nothing to mark the grave but a patch of loose dirt and the marks of his digging, and by the time that he found it the sun was beginning to rise and an aura of soft amber light had appeared at the edge of the fields. Any minute now, Lemuel decided, the ground would split open and his brother would appear. Lowering himself to his knees on the soft dirt, he peered at the ground where Elias lay buried, inspecting the earth for the least sign of change. As he knelt there, he gradually became aware of the sound of someone breathing. When he looked up, a little dark-haired man in a long tatty raincoat and baggy tweed trousers was standing in the half-light not a dozen feet from the grave.

"Lost your spectacles have you, Boyo? Or are you searching for gold dust?" he chuckled. Sitting down on a rock with his long coat spreading out around him, he pulled a mickey of rye from the pocket of his trousers and took a long, hearty swig.

"There's daft you are," he continued, "just like your old grandpa! Scratching about in the dirt like a hedgehog! Is that all you can think of to do with your life?"

Before Lemuel could find words with which to reply to the Welshman, his attention was distracted by a sudden commotion from the direction of his farmhouse. Standing up and squinting into the dawning sun, he could see the hazy, backlit forms of Elias' disciples running toward him, and hear their voices echoing over the lifeless, barren earth.

"Father Elias!" they chanted, kicking up dust clouds as they scampered across the furrows. "Father Elias will be born again! The Resurrection is at hand!"

When Lemuel looked back toward the spot where the Welshman had been sitting, he discovered that the little man had disappeared. Around the rock on which he'd sat, however, the earth was changing colour: tiny blades of jade-green grass were protruding up out of the earth. Lemuel could hardly believe what he was seeing: something was finally growing on his farm! Throwing his arms up toward heaven in jubilation, he ran across the fields that were rapidly turning green all around him to share the joyous news with Elias' disciples, feeling as happy and free as he had as a child on his grandfather's farm. Before he could reach the dark shapes who chanted and shrieked in the distance, however, his feet seemed to stick to the soil of the pasture; he froze to the earth with his still arms uplifted; green buds shot up from the tips of his fingers; his gnarled legs took root in the soft, emerald ground.

Ichthus

Blicter was dreaming. He was floating along on a vast shiny surface, the colour of burnished bronze blazing with sunlight, its depths mined with fissures of luminous fire.

You are dying, a voice said, adrift in the sulphurous air far above him. Hyperborian winds roared and sang in his ears.

As Blicter reached out to steady himself on the surface, his arm struck something solid. The streaming golden sea congealed and formed a waking wall.

God, I was out there a long time, just drifting, he thought, staring at his hand. It was puffy and white, as if bloated from drifting along in the water. He made a fist.

Elaina was sleeping on her back beside him. *When we sleep on our backs*, he thought, *we dream. All of us do. Ergo, she must be dreaming.* The thought of her dreaming calmed him, stilled him. There was something comforting about being part of a community of dreamers, as opposed to being simply at the mercy of one's dreams.

Blicter was thirsty. He climbed out of bed, arching his body over his sleeping wife, being careful not to wake her. When he opened the door of the bedroom, he could see that the rest of the cabin was already flooded with light. It must be nine or ten o'clock, he thought, looking around for the electric clock, which was, of course, fifty miles away at his home in Nanaimo. The cabin, still unfamiliar to him, seemed absurdly ill-equipped and inconvenient. *It's like a goddamn children's playhouse, this cabin*, he decided. *Alice in Wonderland for a hundred and fifty a week.* Locating a glass on a shelf in the kitchen, he rummaged around in the ancient fridge for a moment, then poured himself some orange juice and padded back to bed.

Elaina had cupped her hands over her breasts. She was making small bird-like sounds in her sleep. Blicter drew back

52

the covers and gently splayed one hand on his wife's warm soft belly. She stirred. Her eyelids fluttered. Her mouth came slowly open.

Someone started pounding at the door.

Cursing, Blicter tugged on his bathrobe and padded back to the front of the cabin, taking care to close the bedroom door behind him. After doing up the sash of his robe and putting on his glasses, he slipped back the night-chain and opened the door.

It was one of the kids from the neighbouring cabins. He had been introduced to some of his new neighbours on the day they'd arrived by Mrs. Flatman, who owned the cabins, but he couldn't put a name to the little boy's face. In any case, all little boys seemed to look the same on summer vacation, like so many plucked chickens in their running shoes and grubby T-shirts. This one was a particularly unappetizing example of the species. His chin was non-existent and his nostrils green with mucous. His narrow feet flapped at the cobblestone walk in their decomposing sneakers. He squinted up at Blicter through a huge pair of tortoise-shell glasses. Through the blackberry stains on his T-shirt a printed message said GOD IS LOVE.

"Dad says to tell you you're coming for dinner," he said, pausing to sniff back the snot in his nostrils. "It's pork chops and salad," he added. "And pickles. Don't be late."

His message delivered, the boy turned and ran through the thick groves of arbutus that surrounded all the cabins. In a moment he had vanished, leaving Blicter to wonder who it was that had invited him for dinner. He strained to remember the faces of the other vacationers in the cabins, but no one came to mind. Giving up, he stepped inside and closed the door.

"Was that Mrs. Flatman?" Elaina yelled from the bedroom. "Did she remember to bring us the curtains for the kitchen?"

Blicter stumbled into the bedroom. Elaina was sitting up cross-legged, warm and golden in the rumpled blankets, pouting into a compact-mirror and tugging at her hair.

"It was just some kid," he muttered, shrugging off the bathrobe. "I think he had us mixed up with some people in another cabin. You know how wingy some kids can get when they're turned loose from school for the summer."

"Grumpy old teacher!" Elaina teased, poking him in the ribcage with the toe of her slipper. "You probably think they should lock them up, or put them in the army for the summer. I bet you were even wingier when you were a little kid."

"Nonsense," Blicter answered, running his hand along her naked calf. "I was born a responsible adult, never had time for childhood. And anyway, kids were much more intelligent in the fifties. That was before TV and video games turned their brains into loaves of white bread."

"Well, what's your excuse, then? Above-ground atomic testing? It's a good thing we don't have any children. They'd probably all have tails."

"All right, Dorothy Parker, that's quite enough dazzling repartee for one morning. Brush your fangs and get your knickers on, we're going for a walk. There's some sea-caves on the south end of the island that I want to have a look at. Johanson used to use one for his services in the thirties. You never know, there might even be some artifacts around."

"Instantly, O Master of the Universe," Elaina said, jumping off the dishevelled bed and scampering into the bathroom. "We'd better not keep the ghost of poor old Gunnar Johanson waiting. Although it's probably been over fifty years since anyone's given him a second thought."

And it would probably be another fifty years before anyone did, if it wasn't for him, Blicter decided. He had never heard of anyone else who had researched the Johanson sect. They were all drawn to the flashier cults, the more charismatic swindlers. Charlatans like Brother Twelve had always been good copy, what with his whip-toting mistress and his famous buried treasure, but there was nothing to interest the newspaper flacks in a nondescript man like Johanson, who had simply wandered into a courthouse one morning and announced that he was God.

*   *   *

Blicter had been teaching History at the High School in Nanaimo ever since he'd got out of college, but his interest in Gunnar Johanson had nothing to do with his career. History, local or otherwise, had never really been one of his major interests. He had taken the subject in college because he had no real aptitude for pure science or engineering, thought law school too expensive, and considered himself too stolid to be successful in the Arts. Observing life was his real vocation, and although he found much to pique his interest in his colleagues and his students, his greatest satisfaction came from meeting true eccentrics—"characters" as he called them—and trying to puzzle out in his mind what really made them tick.

Luckily for Blicter, the west coast had its share of eccentrics, especially among the old-time residents, many of whom had come out to the coast to escape the strictures of their religion or their families and to indulge in their curious lifestyles in the privacy of the bush. The myriad of islands in the strait between the mainland and Nanaimo had always been a favourite spot for those who sought tranquillity or who were simply anti-social. Over the years, they'd provided a haven for a dazzling variety of the more exotic Canadian fauna, and it sometimes seemed to Blicter that one could hardly pull in at a sheltered cove or knock at the door of a moss-covered cabin without coming face to face with the last of the Romanoffs or a disciple of Aleister Crowley. The most intriguing of these, in Blicter's eyes, were those who adhered to obscure religions or who claimed to be the avatars of what would soon be worldwide faiths. Of these, quite a few were famous, including Brother Twelve and such flamboyant con-men, but there were others who had remained unknown to all but their immediate neighbours, and who had left no permanent record in the annals of the coast. The most obscure of all was undoubtedly the visionary Gunnar Johanson, of whom not a word was written in all the files in the Provincial Archives, through which Blicter had been carefully picking his way for years.

Blicter had first heard of Johanson from a woman named Trixie Atkins. Trixie was something of a "character" herself, having earned her keep as everything from the matron of a snooty girls' school to a fry-cook in the Yukon, and had retired to a rustic cottage on the north end of Saltspring Island, in which she held court every afternoon from May until September, telling fanciful tales and swilling Bloody Marys by the score. She was a fount of information about the lives of all of her neighbours, knew everyone who lived on the islands, would invent what she couldn't remember, and had been living in the area for years. Blicter had been a regular visitor at Trixie's cottage for several summers, arriving each year at the end of June with a bottle of Russian vodka, content to sit on the shady porch overlooking the channel and listen to the old girl talk.

"I once saw a man walk on water," she confided to Blicter one Dominion Day weekend. "It was on one of those little islands somewheres north of Gabriola. He was an old guy called Gunnar Johanson, had a beard like the Jew of Malta. He was living in some scroungy cave with a couple of crazy bitches. There was half a dozen others, too, who claimed to be the old fool's disciples. Been out under the moon without a hat on one time too many, if you ask me."

That was all that Trixie had ever devulged, having wearied of the subject, but the story stayed in Blicter's mind like a grain of sand inside an oyster, covering itself in images of an old man alone in a sea-cave, an old man who walked on the skin of the sea like an ice-skater skimming down a river. Eventually that old man's life had become Blicter's private obsession. He had roamed the Gulf Islands in his camper every summer, mingling with the Indians and the hippies and the tourists, gradually assembling a detailed file on Gunnar Johanson, a file that he hoped to turn into a best-selling book some day.

And what better place could there be to write such a book than on Gunnar Johanson's island? It had taken him a few years to track it down and to locate the sites where old Johanson had actually been living, but once he had accomplished this, he knew he had to spend an entire summer vacation in the place. Mrs. Flatman's cabins, despite their exorbitant rates, had been a godsend. They were the only accommodation available on the island, and Elaina had categorically refused to spend another summer sleeping cooped up in the camper. She would report him to Amnesty International, she had told him, if he so much as brought the matter up. She had quite liked the idea of living in a cabin for their holiday, however, and had even allowed herself to be talked into coming along on Blicter's research expeditions, a pursuit with which she was, quite understandably, fed up.

The sea-caves, however, were an immediate success. The moment she saw them, Elaina let out an involuntary whoop of delight.

"They're like something out of *Lord Of The Rings*," she said, scrambling down the path ahead of Blicter. "I can just imagine Frodo and the Gollum holed up in these."

"I doubt we'll find anyone quite that exotic, even if it is the tourist season. Would you settle for some cormorants, or some not-very-housebroken gulls?"

The side of the cliff into which the caves were recessed was bleached white with the droppings of sea birds. The scragends of what looked like some rather untidy birdsnests protruded from a few of the less accessible clefts in the worn sandstone rock of the cliff face. A few bedraggled seagulls, apparently the new inhabitants of what had once been Johanson's grotto, wheeled high above the promontory at the south end of the island, mewling plaintively at Blicter and Elaina.

"Be careful," Blicter yelled ahead to his wife as they inched along the narrow path that was notched into the cliff-face, and immediately regretted having said it. She would think that he was simply trying to play the protective male, and resent the implication of weakness. And it was ridiculous, really, for him to worry about her. Despite the mane of platinum curls and the starved-to-perfection figure, she had always been a tomboy with a love of the outdoors, and could run rings around him at anything athletic. If anyone took a header off the cliff, it would be him. And *he* couldn't walk on water, like old Johanson.

Unlike the majority of the other caves that Blicter had explored on the islands, Johanson's caves were well above the reach of even the highest tides, and were sheltered by a lip of rock from all but the harshest winds. Still, it was difficult for Blicter and Elaina to imagine, as they poked their heads into one cave after another and peered into the shadowy recesses, that anyone, even a crazy man, could have lived in such a place.

"How did he keep himself warm?" Elaina asked, squirming her way under a heavy rock outcrop above the mouth of the largest cavern. "And what did they do when they got hungry in this place? Pick up the phone and order a pizza?"

"Johanson was fasting during most of his time here—keeping his weight down, I would imagine, for his strolls across the briny. And as for his womenfolk, I suppose they came and went. Even messiahs must get boring in the long run."

Having successfully negotiated the narrow gap beneath the outcrop, Elaina suddenly disappeared into the interior of the cave, and Blicter found himself talking to a ridge of pitted stone, which looked as if it had heard it all before. It occurred to him, as he wedged himself between the cavern wall and the jagged knob of limestone, sucking in his modest paunch and trying not to think about bats and spiders, that Johanson himself must have wormed his way under this very same rock perhaps a thousand times back in the thirties. What significance would this ragged cleft have had in the mind of such a man, a man who was said to have earnestly believed that he himself was God, and that everything he saw and touched was holy? While the Freudian interpretation was obvious, and immediately occurred to Blicter, it seemed unlikely that

58

Johanson, with his grade school education, had ever heard about psychoanalysis, let alone about Sigmund Freud. But perhaps he *would* have seen the cave as a womb, if only in his subconscious, and had sought it out instinctively as a haven and a refuge, the perfect place for a simple man who yearned to be reborn. Or perhaps it was just that the cave's narrow mouth would keep the rain from blowing in, and keep him sheltered from the prying eyes of tourists on their boats. Besides, it was the only cave that was big enough to live in for any length of time. And you certainly couldn't bitch about the taxes.

"Have you considered the Scarsdale diet?" Elaina said, as he finally wormed his way under the rock and emerged in the inner chamber of the cavern. She was standing in a slight depression in the centre of the cave, looking up into the shaft of sunlight that was streaming from a hole in the limestone ceiling, where a fissure in the rock had formed a sort of natural chimney. The rock around the oblong hole was black with ash and soot, and there was a corresponding dark patch in the dip where Elaina stood.

"A smokehole," Blicter whispered. "Well, that explains how he kept warm. Now if we could only find the cablevision hook-up."

"Philistine," Elaina muttered, turning her back on Blicter. "I would have thought that even an empty-headed vassal of the Ministry of Education would feel a certain *frisson* in a holy place like this."

"Are you referring to the hole in the roof or to the fact that Johanson lived here? I rather doubt that having had a lunatic in residence for a year or two back in the thirties would be enough to put this troglodyte's dream into the same class as St. Paul's Cathedral. On the other hand, who am I to have an opinion on such a lofty subject? Perhaps old Gunnar really *was* a god, and made that hole with a bolt of lightning? Stranger things have happened, or so they tell us in the *National Enquirer*."

"What are you being so defensive about? You know I was

59

only joking. And it was *you* who wanted to spend the summer researching this Johanson. It would certainly never occur to me to spend a whole summer peering into caves."

She was right, Blicter decided. He was being a pain in the backside. Why did he have to put on a show of scepticism about Johanson? No one had ever accused him of believing in the silly old duffer. And Elaina had been so understanding, so indulgent about his interest in the coast and its eccentrics. Plenty of women would have told him what to do with his research. In an effort to make amends, he went over to her and touched her shoulder, looping his arm around her waist and trying to pull her close. She was preoccupied, however, with something she'd discovered on the wall of the cavern. She stroked at the rock with the tips of her fingers, brushing loose dirt from the surface.

"Look at this," she whispered, stepping aside to let Blicter examine the smooth stone of the wall. "Could it possibly be connected with Johanson?"

Scratched into the porous stone was the shape of a tiny fish. Its outline was unmistakable, despite the years of dust and dampness.

"*Ichthus*," Blicter whispered. "The sign of the Roman Christians. They used it in the time of St. Paul as a symbol for their religion. I suppose old man Johanson must have decided to adopt it. They're never very original though, are they, these new messiahs? They always seem to be dredging up all the old reliable props."

Elaina wasn't listening. She had retreated to the centre of the cavern again and was looking up intently at the shaft of light from the smokehole. She had folded her arms beneath her breasts and seemed to be hugging herself as she stood there, a pose which could in another context have been seen as anything from matronly to seductive, but which in this instance seemed unmistakably an expression of fear.

"Stuffy in here, isn't it?" Blicter said lamely. Then, striding over to the narrow cleft through which they had entered, he added, "I don't know about you, but I could use a bite of something. Let's go see if those blasted gulls have made off with our lunch."

The clouds had burned off while they had been inside the cavern, and the sea had turned a glorious blue and was as smooth as a piece of china. Having made their way out of Johanson's cave and clambered to the top of the cliff-face, Blicter and Elaina sprawled out in the tremulous shade of a pair of gnarled arbutus and shared their picnic lunch. For a long time they were silent, content to watch the marbled sea and the mountains of the mainland, and to listen to the mewling of the ever-present gulls. It was Elaina who broke the silence, lifting herself up on her knees in the tufts of grass and looking quizzically at Blicter.

"Who were the women?" she asked, shredding a mottled arbutus leaf that had fluttered to earth beside her.

"The women with Johanson? The ones who lived in that cave, you mean?" Blicter answered, squinting up at her.

She nodded.

"Don't know much about them, really. One had a name like Posthewaite, or Thistlethorpe, or something. The other had been a postal clerk in some whistlestop on the mainland. Life must have been pretty dreadful for the pair of them before they came here, I would imagine, to make living in a hole with a holy man seem like a good idea."

He stood up and brushed the dried bits of grass from his T-shirt and trousers.

"We'd better head back to the cabin," he said, picking up the picnic basket. "We still have to get some milk and stuff, and a lightbulb for the bathroom, and that goddamn store down by the government dock is closed by half past four."

Elaina regarded the long thorny spine of the leaf she'd been shredding.

"Do you think they were in love with him?" she asked, standing up and taking the basket from her husband.

"With Johanson? God knows. Sure as hell couldn't have been after his money. The old bugger didn't have a penny to his name."

"It must have been fun in a way, though, living out here like cavemen. I wonder if they lived on roots and berries from the bushes. Or maybe they gathered eggs and things. Or hunted with bows and arrows. Can you imagine going home at night and gnawing on a seagull? Remember that stupid movie we saw with all those sleazy-looking cavemen? They reminded me of the tourists on the ferry from Nanaimo. Take away the cameras and things and you couldn't tell the difference. We really don't need that cabin, you know, we could come here and live in the caves."

Laughing, Elaina slumped over until her knuckles brushed the sea grass, and then thrust her narrow jaw forward and started to chatter like a monkey. The charade was made more ridiculous by her blonde hair and delicate features. Such slapstick seemed out of place, somehow, in such a classically beautiful woman. Yet her inability to take herself seriously was a quality that Blicter had always found particularly attractive. He leaned against a tree and grinned to himself as she shambled away down the pathway. Her mood-shifts left him breathless, made him feel somehow dull and clumsy. Only a moment before she had looked as if those gloomy caves had spooked her, as if she were upset by all his talk about that loony old Johanson, and now she was leaping around in the woods like a female Buster Keaton. How different she seemed from the wretched girls who had lived in that cave with Johanson. What pathetic, spineless creatures they must have been, to waste their lives on a madman like him.

Blicter suddenly felt an almost physical need to get away from Johanson's caverns. After all the painstaking research it had taken him to find the caves, the reality of seeing them had filled him with a queasy numbness. That was why he had been so determined to laugh the whole thing off, to make a joke of it. His mind had been filled with images of that old man and his girlfriends, curled up in that hole in the ground like a brace of pallid cave-newts, delirious with the worship of their imaginary god.

Glancing nervously over his shoulder, he trotted down the

path after Elaina. In a moment he had caught up to her and relieved her of the clumsy picnic basket. They walked home through the sunlight to their cabin on the beach.

*　　*　　*

"You do like your daddy told you. Go on. Them people won't bite you. Go on. Ring the doorbell."

"They don't *put* doorbells on a cabin."

"Go knock on the door them. Go on. Not the screen door, the *real* door."

"*Mom!*"

"Hurry up now. Them pork chops is going to be burned to a frazzle."

Blicter rolled over onto his back in the narrow, uncomfortable cot in the bedroom of the cabin. He rubbed the sleep from his eyes for a moment, then put on his glasses and sat up on the edge of the bed. The bickering voices at the front door grew louder, as raucous as a whole flock of crows in a tree.

"Geez Mom, I asked them already this morning. Maybe they're sick and they don't feel like eating."

"They could of forgotten. It's hours since you asked them. Go on. Ring the doorbell. They're likely asleep."

The screen door creaked open. There was a hesitant knocking.

"Elaina," Blicter croaked. His mouth tasted foul and his throat was constricted. He was muddled and sluggish from falling asleep in the heat of early evening. His wife didn't answer, and after awhile he distinguished the hiss of the primitive shower in the bathroom from the chatter of birds and the sound of the waves washing in on the sandy beach in front of the cabin. A bead of sweat arced down the curve of his ribcage. He put on his bathrobe and went to the door.

It was the same kid who had asked him to dinner that morning. He had apparently found time to go swimming in the interval between his mysterious visits to the door of Blicter's cabin, as his dark hair was plastered to his head like a skullcap and a pair of rubber diving goggles dangled from his

63

neck. A thickset woman in a shapeless print housedress and pink rubber sandals was hovering in the shade of an arbutus tree behind him.

"Go on. Go on. Ask him," she prompted, frowning at the youngster. "You won't get nothing done in this world if you don't take the bull by the horns."

The boy flushed and looked from the woman to Blicter.

"My dad says you're supposed to be coming for dinner. My mom cooked the pork chops. You coming or what?"

Blicter took his glasses off and wiped his brow with the sleeve of his bathrobe. He couldn't think of a word to say to the scrawny boy or the woman. Embarrassed by his awkwardness, he stepped back in the room and called out once again for Elaina. He was greeted by a gust of damp air as she opened the door of the bathroom.

"Are you dying to pee?" she said, emerging from a cloud of steam, her hair wrapped in a towel. "Oh Christ," she added, catching sight of the boy. "Didn't realize we had company. Aren't you going to ask them in?"

"Sorry. Of course," he said, relieved to see that Elaina was wearing her housecoat and hadn't stepped out of the bathroom stark naked. "Forgive me. Won't you come in and sit down. I think we have some lemonade and a beer or two in the fridge. Come in and have a drink while we get dressed, and then we'll have a chance to get acquainted."

The woman grinned and waved but made no move toward the door. The boy just yawned and fiddled with his goggles.

"It seems," Blicter said, "that our new neighbours have invited us for dinner."

"Dinner?" Elaina whispered, retreating toward the bedroom. "How kind of them." She rolled her eyes. "Will you just give me a minute to put my clothes on?" She made a face and hissed at him, then closed the bedroom door, leaving Blicter standing helpless in the hallway.

"We'll, ah, be with you in a minute," he told the boy, resigning himself to an evening of small talk. "Are you sure you won't come in?" he added, forcing himself to smile. When neither replied, he stalked into the bedroom.

"Brilliant!" Elaina whispered, as soon as he'd closed the door. "Couldn't you have told them we have leprosy or something? Did you see that awful woman? And the kid looks like he has rickets. I think I saw the pair of them playing banjoes in *Deliverance*. What on earth could possibly have possessed you to accept?"

"It wasn't a matter of accepting, really. That boy came around this morning. When he showed up again a few minutes ago, I was zoned out in the bedroom. By the time I got my head together, it was too late to refuse them. And anyway, it's not so bad. They're only trying to be friendly. We'll have a quick drink and press the flesh and bugger off back home."

He dragged a suitcase from under the bed and rummaged around in it until he found a clean shirt and a fresh pair of shorts. He put them on and stepped into his soiled baggy trousers, the same ones he'd worn to the sea caves that morning, checked his back pocket to make sure he had his wallet, took the key from the windowsill and opened the bedroom door.

"Do you think we should take a salad?" he asked. "Or a bottle of wine or something? We still have that bottle of Mouton-Cadet that we forgot to take along on the picnic."

"Yes. Yes. Anything. Give them nuclear waste for all I care. Just go outside and entertain them while I try to find something to wear."

"All right. But do try to hurry. It sounds as though we're holding up their dinner as it is," Blicter said. He took the bottle of wine from the cupboard in the kitchen, then went outside to make conversation with the woman and the boy.

"I thought I'd bring some plonk along," he said to the woman, smiling and holding up the bottle. "Does red go with pork chops? I never could remember. We drink this stuff with anything, although Elaina prefers the white."

The woman nodded vaguely and looked off toward the shoreline. The boy had put his goggles on and was stalking through the sea grass. His rubber mask and spindly limbs gave him the appearance of an insect, like some interstellar mutant in a science fiction film.

Seeing Blicter on the doorstep, he stopped playing and turned toward him, a shaft of sunlight gleaming on his protruding, alien eyes.

"Is she coming or what?" he whined. "We've been waiting for hours. Them chops'll be blacker than hockey pucks by now."

At that moment Elaina appeared in the doorway. She had put on a pair of satin shorts and a sleeveless pink top that revealed her bare shoulders. Her eyes were concealed behind wire-rimmed dark glasses.

"Sorry to be so long," she said, linking arms with Blicter. "Introduce me to your friends," she added, nudging him with her elbow.

Blicter was embarrassed to realize that he hadn't introduced himself, or even thought to ask the boy and the woman who they were. Before he could attempt to rectify this oversight, however, the strangers turned their backs on him and walked toward the shoreline, heading for the worn path that led to the other cabins. There was nothing left for him and Elaina to do but tag along.

At the end of the long row of neatly-painted cabins, the couple ahead of them wandered off the narrow path and began to pick their way through the tangle of arbutus trees and salal on the hill between the shoreline and the road from the government dock. Cursing under her breath, Elaina took off her high-heeled sandals and reluctantly started to climb through the scrub brush. By the time she finally reached the road she had scratches on her bare legs and there were bits of leaves adhering to the soft material of her top. Blicter climbed up behind her, breathing heavily in the heat.

"Is it very much farther?" he yelled to the woman, who had set off down the gravel road with the boy at her side. "We assumed that you were staying at the cabins."

"Can't afford no fancy cabins," she answered. "The husband has his camper truck. We been living down the road here in the camper since last winter. We got it on some government land, right down here on the water. You have to take the roadway because there's rocks between us and them cabins. Unless you wait till the tide goes down, and then you can walk on the beach."

Elaina shot Blicter a plaintive look and nodded in the direction of the shoreline. While he was aware that she wanted desperately to turn back and go home to the safety of their cabin, to get away from these ridiculous and faintly unnerving people, the woman's revelations about her husband and his camper had awakened his curiosity, and he was reluctant to go back. She certainly was a "character," he reflected, watching her as she stumped along the crude gravel road through the sunlight, her rubber sandals slapping at her bare feet as she walked. And he was anxious to meet her husband, to whom she seemed so deferrential. The guy must really be a winner, he decided, almost as bad as old Johanson. Just imagine someone squatting on government land all winter, probably getting along without electricity or water, cooped up in a camper with that woman and her idiot son. Ignoring Elaina's obvious reluctance, he started down the road after the woman, suddenly looking forward to this dinner with their newfound friends. Putting on her heels again, Elaina limped along behind him, grabbing his arm to steady herself as she stumbled on the gravel. About a quarter of an hour later, they finally reached the woman's camp.

It was even worse that Blicter and Elaina had expected. The "camper" was an old Dodge truck with a windowless box on its flatbed. A tent was pitched beside it, with a few wooden chairs and a table. A hollow-cheeked man in a nylon windbreaker was sitting at the table, gazing absently at the rusted portable barbeque that was standing beside the truck. He looked up through the smoke as his wife walked toward him.

"Them pork chops is done to a turn," he said, standing up and smiling at Blicter and Elaina. "Real glad you could come here and join us," he added. "My name's Harold Phelps and my wife's name is Katherine. The boy is called Geoffrey. Sit down, have a chair."

Blicter and Elaina introduced themselves and perched hesitantly on the flimsy-looking chairs beside the table. The boy disappeared into the back of the camper while the woman fussed with the barbeque and laid out the plates and glasses.

"Thought you might like some wine with dinner," Blicter said, proferring the bottle. "It's probably a little on the warm side, I'm afraid."

"Don't take to drink as a rule," the man said. He sat down and took the bottle. "But I'll have a short one all the same, just to be polite."

He fished a jack-knife from the pocket of his windbreaker, fiddled with its intricate blades for a moment until he located a miniature corkscrew, then deftly drew the cork.

"Like getting a pig out of a goddamn mouse-hole," he said, winking at Elaina. He poured them each a glass of wine. "Now Ma there," he added, nodding toward the woman, "she'd as soon be flayed alive as touch a drop of this here liquor. Signed the pledge before she was twelve. And took it literal, not like some folk."

He drained his glass in a single gulp and smacked his lips with pleasure.

"Great one for the religion, my missus," he sighed.

The woman put a china bowl full of lettuce leaves and quartered tomatoes on the table.

"You can help yourselves to salad," she said. She plonked a jar of Miracle Whip on the table beside the salad. "There's only four pork chops and they're fried up to nothing. Hope nobody's hungry. I would have bought six, but they come four to a packet. That woman at the grocery store won't let you just buy two."

She put the pork chops on a plate and placed them on the table. It was obvious, after a moment, that no one was going to take one.

"It's too damn hot for chops," the man said, reaching for the bottle. He poured himself a glass of wine and downed it in a swallow. "Give the blasted things to that son of yours. These folks would just as soon have salad."

The woman picked up the plate of chops and walked off toward the camper. The man filled Blicter's glass with wine and poured himself another.

"This is something she takes a mind to do every now and again," he confided. "Fixes up a batch of food and feeds it to some strangers. Thinks its the Christian thing to do, feeding people you don't know from Adam. I suppose it makes her feel like she's a half-assed goddamn saint."

"It's very kind of you," Blicter muttered, looking nervously at Elaina. He picked up a fork and speared a slice of ripe tomato. "Have some salad, Dear?" he asked his wife, pushing the bowl toward her.

Elaina shot him a poisonous look and pulled her chair up to the table.

"I'd be interested to hear your views about religion, Mr. Phelps," she said, smiling demurely and opening her lovely blue eyes very wide. "My husband and I have been developing an interest in the subject. We're researching a man named Johanson, who lived here in the thirties. He used to have a church of sorts, on the south end near the water. Perhaps you've heard of him? They say he could walk on water. Perhaps you should suggest that to your ever-so-saintly wife."

"Never met the man," Phelps said cautiously. He seemed to sense that Elaina was mocking him, but was uncertain how he should react. He gulped his wine and gently put the glass back on the table. "Got some bingo in the truck," he said. He stood up and made his way unsteadily toward the camper. There was a flurry of angry voices from inside the box of the camper, then Phelps lurched back toward them with a gallon jug in his hand.

"Any hooer'll do'er, eh?" Phelps said, as he removed the screw top. "This may not taste like your fancy stuff, but it'll do the same job in the long run."

The jug was full of murky fluid, with bits of sediment floating near the bottom. Phelps poured himself and Blicter a drink, then cocked an eyebrow at Elaina.

"Can I offer you a blast?" he asked.

Elaina gave him an icy look, then began to search around for her handbag.

"Ah well, you suit yourself," he drawled. "Now tell me more about this friend of yours, the one who can walk on the salt chuck."

"Johanson, you mean," Blicter said. "It's a fascinating story, really," he added, warming to his subject. He was about to tell the man about his research into the Johanson cult, but before he could he was interrupted by Elaina.

"Don't you think it's time we left?" she said. Her voice was tight with anger. She got up and started to walk toward the road.

"But I was just telling Mr. Phelps—"

"Harold, goddamn it. Call me Harold."

"—I was just telling Harold about this Johanson thing, Elaina. I'm sure he'd like to hear about our trip out to the sea caves. Why don't you sit down and relax for a minute and have a glass of wine?"

"You can stay if you want," Elaina said. "I'm tired. I have a headache."

She walked a few unsteady steps up the trail through the gathering twilight, then stopped and turned around again, as if waiting for Blicter to follow.

"Are you sure it's all right if I stay?" he asked. "I can catch you up in a couple of minutes."

He took a hesitant sip of Phelps' wine, made a sour face, and started to chuckle.

"Of course I don't mind," Elaina replied. "You just stay here with good old Harold. He'll look good in your collection, right next to old Johanson. You can dip him in formaldehyde and nail him to a board."

She turned and walked as quickly as her fragile heels allowed her up the trail to the road. In a moment she had vanished through the gap between the trees.

"Lovely woman, your wife," Phelps said. He raked his hands through his sparse grey hair. "Tell me more about this goddamn Johanson."

Blicter needed no further encouragement. He leaned back in the uncomfortable wooden chair and began to tell Phelps about his research. He had always considered himself to be something of a raconteur, and he embellished his story with anecdotes and impressions, mimicking the throaty voice of his old friend Trixie Atkins and acting out his difficult entry through the door of Johanson's cave. The sun had finally set behind the islands in the distance, and its last light cast a shining path across the glassy water. At times like this, Blicter slyly observed, you could almost believe in Johanson. How easy it would be to walk down to the shore and set your foot on that long gleaming pathway. He could almost see that bearded old man with his arms stretched out to heaven, walking into the waning light across a sea of burning gold, his disciples kneeling reverently at the shoreline.

As Blicter spoke, Phelps slumped down in his chair and listened in sullen silence. Every few minutes he poured himself another glass of wine, and downed it with an air of self-destructive violence. When Blicter finished his story, Phelps stood up, knocking over his chair. He cleared his throat and spat a gob of phlegm into the fire.

"My goddamn old woman could do that," he said. He started to walk unsteadily toward the camper. A few minutes later he came staggering back toward Blicter, leading his sleep-fuddled son by the arm.

"Old cow says she's too goddamn tired to come out of the camper. Over-exerted herself, she says, fixing the dinner. The kid and her were flaked out in the goddamn truck asleep."

The boy's face was puffy with sleep under his sunburn. His damp hair had dried while he slept and was matted on one side and frizzy on the other. He had taken off his shoes and socks, and his feet looked pale and dirty. He stumbled along docilely behind his drunken father, as if he were used to being dragged out of bed.

"This boy here's religious," Phelps slurred. "His mom raised him proper. He can walk on the goddamn sea just like your friend."

71

He started to drag the boy down the slope toward the water. Blicter, unsure as to how seriously he should take this performance, remained in his seat and watched them as they weaved toward the beach. He suspected that Phelps, in his drunkenness, was making fun of his obsession with Johanson, punishing him for insisting on telling his story in such detail. He had, he decided, been tactless. He realized that he could be a bore when he got on his favourite subject. He shouldn't assume that others would share his interest in eccentrics. He would apologize to Phelps for boring him, and then he would head back to the cabin. Elaina would be there by now, and would worry if he stayed out too long.

Both Phelps and the boy were standing up to their ankles in the water. The boy stared at his father with a look of numb incomprehension, like a dog that has grown used to being struck for no good reason. The man was making gestures in the direction of the dark horizon, as if he were attempting to describe some point of interest on one of the islands in the distance. As Blicter approached, he turned around and climbed back up onto the gravel, leaving his son to stand bewildered in the wash of the incoming tide.

"Useless as tits on a chicken," he said. He staggered up the gravel beach and plunged into the scrub brush beside it. In a moment he emerged again, brandishing a thin forked alder branch, from which he was clumsily stripping the leaves.

"I'll teach you to embarrass me," he growled. "You're as bad as your goddamn mother. Turn your nose up at your own flesh and blood and spout your damn religion. Let's see you walk to Vancouver then, you gutless little bugger."

He flailed with the branch at the water, driving his son out away from the shoreline. The boy retreated until the waves began to wash around his shoulders, then started to thrash his arms and legs in a sort of childish dog-paddle. For a moment he swam along parallel to the beach, staring tearfully at his staggering father, then he turned his head and began to swim laboriously out to sea.

His anger spent, Phelps dropped his branch and took a few clumsy steps backward.

"That kid can't swim worth coon shit," he said. He sat down with a sudden thud on a log beside the water and began to vomit soundlessly down the front of his thin plaid shirt.

Blicter realized that the boy was in danger of drowning. He was drained from his long day out in the hot sun and drowsy with the strong homemade wine he'd been drinking, and the events of the last few minutes seemed to have had a tinge of unreality, like something dreamed or half-remembered. He slapped and shook the stupified Phelps, trying desperately to make him comprehend the seriousness of the situation, but the drunken man remained slumped on his log, oblivious to everything around him. It gradually dawned on Blicter that it was up to him to save the boy.

Everything had seemed to be happening too fast; now everything happened too slowly. He fumbled leaden-fingered with the buttons of his shirt, took an age to kick his sandals off, became entangled with the recalcitrant zipper on his trousers. By the time he waded into the sea, the waves were serene and placid. There was no sign of the flailing boy, no sound but the shriek of seagulls.

He stretched out on the gentle swells and began to swim into the darkness. The waves rolled in to meet him and the cold water cleared his senses. He had only the vaguest idea of where the boy had been when he'd last seen him, and he was pierced by a growing awareness that the youngster must have already drowned. He was also aware, however, that he would continue to search for the boy until he no longer had the strength to swim or tread water. And he was aware that when he finally gave up the search, as eventually he would have to, he would take home with him the knowledge that he was responsible for the death of this stranger. The eccentricity that had so intrigued him he now recognized as madness; the boy seemed a kind of sacrifice to the dark gods whom he had provoked.

As he circled a few dozen yards from the shore where Phelps was still hunched in the darkness, putting off the inevitable moment when he would have to go back and wake him, Blicter remembered the dream that he'd had that morning. He saw again the golden sea and floated on its shining surface. But now he knew what the dream had meant and how it would have ended. He would have felt himself begin to sink beneath a surface that could not support him. He would have felt the waters close above his body and engulf it. And then he would be lost forever in the depths of the limitless ocean, falling and falling through the echoing dark.

The Tale of
the Ratcatcher's Daughter

Later, when the universe had narrowed to a single sphere of lamplight and he felt as if his soul were being dragged out of his body, Boy Fury would remember his father's advice.

"There's no God up in heaven who can help you when you're down at the bottom of a coal mine," the old man had whispered, squinting as if blinded by the light of his own wisdom, "but you won't know who you are, my boy, until you've been alone down in that mine."

When Boy's father had been a foreman in the coal mine in Nanaimo, he had often doused the kerosene lantern on the top of his miner's helmet when he was all by himself at the bottom of the mineshaft. Standing in the darkness with his back against the coal seam, with the whole damn planet heaving and groaning all around him, he would laugh into the absolute blackness of the abyss, like some unrepentant Titan whom the gods had sealed in stone.

After Boy's father had bought all the mines around Nanaimo, of course, he had better things to do than to go down into the mineshafts. He left that to his miners.

And to the ratcatcher, Mr. Death.

Mr. Death had been a parson in some village in New England. He had turned up in Nanaimo on a listing Boston clipper, with a suitcase full of whiskey bottles and his beautiful blue-eyed daughter, as homeless as an angel who has dropped out of a cloud.

Taking pity on the defrocked parson, Boy's father had given him a menial job in the paymaster's office at one of his coal mines. He had drunk his way out of that job, and out of half a dozen others, before eventually descending to his present occupation: setting traps for the blind rats that lived down in the mines.

Boy's childhood had been haunted by the thought of that drunken Yankee preacher. In his nightmares he would see the ratcatcher rising from the mouth of the coal mine, mangled rats dangling by their tails from his belt-loops, his kerosene lantern gleaming like a cyclopean eye. Every shadow that swam across the walls of his bedroom, every whisper of wind in the trees outside the window, every rumble that came echoing through the steam pipes in the ceiling seemed to signal the inevitable approach of Mr. Death.

As Boy's mother had died while giving birth to him, he had largely been raised by a nurse whom his father had imported from the Scottish highlands, a rodent-eyed old woman by the name of Nanny Goodwin. It was she who tucked Boy in at night in the absence of his mother. It was she who read him excerpts from the works of Rudyard Kipling. And it was she who told him about the drunkard who'd gone to live down in the coal mine, and about his blue-eyed daughter, the most beautiful girl who had ever set foot in the village of Nanaimo, with golden hair and skin like silk and cheeks like summer roses.

Whose name, as Boy remembered, had been Pearly.

Pearly Death.

If Boy had lived in fear of ever coming face-to-face with that defrocked parson, he lived in hope of meeting up with the ratcatcher's beautiful daughter. She filled his dreams like water fills the hollows in a stone floor, flowing through an emptiness of which he was only just aware.

But it was unlikely, to be honest, that Boy would ever see that parson *or* his daughter, as he had spent his entire life within the walls of his father's house.

That house had been an absolute obsession to Boy's father. While hunting in the hills above Nanaimo one foggy morning, he had stumbled on a coal seam half the width of Vancouver Island. Transformed in an instant from the commonest of labourers into the wealthiest man in the whole of the province, he had decided to build a monument to his incredible good fortune: a house that was as infinite as the creations of the Lord.

The house had taken years to build, and was never really finished. No sooner would a new wing be completed than the floor in an older one would crumble, rotted prematurely by the dampness of the climate. Ornamental gardens which had taken months of painstaking labour to build would subside without warning into the labyrinths of abandoned mineshafts that honeycombed the hillsides around the village, leaving soggy lunar craters in which only crabgrass and nettles would grow. Douglas fir would sprout up like weeds in the soil of the sheltered courtyards, their huge roots rending the roman tile walks and shivering the stained glass doors. It was difficult to tell, at times, whether the legions of carpenters and stone-masons who worked for Boy's father were building a mansion, or tearing one apart.

Not that any of these difficulties seemed to matter to Boy's father. Oblivious to the problems presented by the landscape, he went right on building and building and building. The house sent out tentacles and expanded its perimeters. Gothic towers and Moroccan minarets reached upward toward heaven. Ships weighed down with granite blocks came floundering into the harbour. Architects came and went through the town like magpies in a birdhouse, each of them proclaiming the virtues of an entirely different design.

And so it was that the house became a galaxy of houses, each one of them embodying a different architectural style.

"Thy father's house has many mansions," Boy's father would tell him, winking and jabbing a thumb at his waistcoat. It was a joke he never tired of, one which his son had heard so often that the words had lost their meaning, just as the house itself had ceased to be a simple human dwelling, and become a sort of universe, with Boy's father its omnipotent God.

It was in this house that Boy was born, and in this house he grew to manhood. Sheltered from the world by the walls of that mansion, encased in the gauzy cocoon of his family, he evolved through the various larval stages of his childhood like some microscopic insect in a glutinous solution, blissfully unaware of any existence save his own. He was the sort of boy you might see dozing in the sunlight on a staircase, absorbed in the limpid translucencies of a sunbeam as it trembled like a living thing across the Persian carpets. Or clumping down the hallways in a sailor suit and a straw boater, clutching the toy ship made of conch shells and ivory that his father had bought from a wandering sailor. Or standing in rooms full of shrouded chairs and tables, gazing into bell-jars from which birds, or bird-like things, gazed back at him with eyes like amber whirlpools. Years drifted past as he lounged in the courtyards. Processions of houseguests filed nattering past doorways. Various personages, who may have been servants, materialized and vanished in the echoing spaces like allegorical figures in some mediaeval pageant, leaving silver trays laden with inscrutable objects. Time itself ground to a halt and stood still.

Eventually, however, Boy began to notice a change in his surroundings. Windows that had shattered were no longer mended. The thick Persian carpets were mildewed and threadbare. Rain poured unhampered through the skylight in the ballroom. The doorbells closed ranks in a conspiracy of silence. The servants became frailer and fewer in number. The last of the builders packed his bags and departed, pausing briefly to spit tobacco juice on the ruins of the doorstep. Everything seemed to be falling apart.

So it was that, one day that seemed inexplicably unlike all the others, Boy finally found himself absolutely alone.

But what on earth had become of his family?

(1) His mother, who claimed to be the daughter of an Anglican Archbishop. So well brought up that she could scarcely breathe the rough air of Nanaimo without falling down unconscious in a perfumed heap on the carpet. Uttered a filmy gout of blood at the moment of Boy's birth and perished.

Her portrait hung like a silent reproach in the gloom of the cavernous parlour.

(2) His ne'er-do-well Uncle Francis, who had run off to join the circus and returned a lifetime later with his cross-eyed bride Conchita from the jungles of Guiana. Retired to the gazebo in the middle of the Japanese gardens, to a life of catching butterflies and reading Vauvenargues. Found in a bed of hibiscus with his skull pierced by a single feather. Conchita packed off to Guiana, furiously protesting her innocence.

(3) His elder sister, Mary, who slept on boards and wore a hairshirt, a crown of thorns and a nail-studded girdle. Given to bellowing hymns at all hours of the day or night, and to clubbing the town drunk with a crucifix. Disappeared into thin air one sunlit afternoon, apparently carried up to heaven.

(4) His other sister, Helen, who slept with anyone who asked her. Whose voice Boy had encountered in the hallways of the mansion, shimmering like moonlight through the saffron-scented spaces. Whom he had seen on rare occasions in the parlour or the alcoves, admiring the curve of her lip in a wineglass or swiping the dust from the tops of her riding boots. Having been given (by her doting Uncle Francis) a biography of Catherine the Great for her sixteenth birthday, attempted to seduce her father's demented Arabian stallion. Her ghost still appears outside the stables to this day, a startled voice hovering in the moonlight.

(5) His horned and shadowed father, who had always seemed more a creature of myth than a living, breathing man to him. Having acquired wealth beyond his wildest dreams instantaneously in the discovery of one mine, lost it just as quickly in the disappearance of another. As their markets were eroded by the use of oil for fuel, the coal mines around Nanaimo had been closing down one by one for the past few decades, and Boy's father had sought to protect his wealth by diversifying

79

his investments. The Flying Dutchman diamond mine, (somewhere) in the Transvaal, was located by a group of prospectors just long enough to attract a few guileless investors, Boy's father among them, before it vanished into legend like its demon-haunted namesake, leaving everyone connected with it in a state of financial ruin.

Boy found his father lying on the cracked stones of the inner courtyard, the barrel of a duelling pistol jammed against his palate, his cerebellum caved in like the shaft of a worked-out mine.

Having idled away half a lifetime in the confines of that labyrinthine mansion, Boy packed a few things in a carpetbag and wandered out the door.

It was raining, raining, raining, raining, raining in the real world.

He had no idea where he was going. He had no idea where there was to go.

That night, as he lay sleeping in the long grass beside the driveway, Boy dreamed that he was searching through the dark depths of a coal mine. He was looking for something he had lost down there, although he couldn't imagine what. Faces from his waking life swam up through the dark to meet him, unchanged by death or absence from the way that he had known them, as if time had frozen solid in the cold depths of that mine. He saw his mother bleeding from her thin lips in the darkness, her eyes as cold as chips of flint and her skin as white as ashes. Uncle Francis strolled by arm in arm with his cross-eyed Conchita, whose hair was stuck full of feathers and who whistled like a bird. Sister Mary shook her head at Boy in saintly disapproval, a bloody cross emblazoned in the centre of her forehead, while Sister Helen transfixed him with a single glance of her scalding green eyes. His father's laugh came echoing through the darkness, darkness, darkness. And a woman's hand wrote *Pearly* in the coal dust on a wall.

When he woke up the next morning, Boy knew exactly

what he had to do. Brushing the bits of hayseed from his shapeless coat and his baggy trousers, Boy set out in the direction of his father's old No. 1 mine. With only the vaguest idea of where the long-abandoned coal mine was located, Boy wandered in the hills above Nanaimo until nightfall, in awe at the wild diversity of a landscape he had only seen in pictures, or in distant glimpses peering from an upstairs window in his father's house. At times he saw the ocean far below him through the pine stands, or felt a breath of salt air in the landward breeze of evening. A thin mist from the mountains shivered down the trees to meet him. Unimaginable birds broke cover as he stumbled up the path.

It was almost dark by the time that Boy finally arrived at the coal mine. No. 1 was in many ways exactly as he'd imagined. The shapes of the sheds and conveyors loomed like dolmens in the half-light. The shadows of the cables spread their wings across the slag-heaps. But the outlines of the buldings had been blurred by weeds and scrub brush, and the wheels and gears were caked with mud and chancred with blood-coloured rust.

It was obvious that No. 1 had not been worked in many years.

So this was what had happened to his father, Boy reflected. The darkness he had mined and sold had finally overwhelmed him. The emptiness had risen from the earth and struck him dead. But it was not the time, he realized, for such fruitless contemplation. He had to find his way down to the bottom of the mineshaft. He could almost see the rheumy eyes of that drunken Boston parson. He could almost feel the golden hair of his daughter, Pearly Death.

As if guided by some instinct that was beyond his comprehension, Boy made his way directly to the iron cage of the mankiller, the lift in which the miners had once been lowered down through the shaft. Boy knew in his bones he had been born for this moment. He opened the door of the cage and stepped inside. Releasing the rusted handbrake, he started his descent.

Dark. Dark, Dark. Dark. Dark. Dark.
Dark. Dark. Dark. Dark. Dark.
Dark. Dark. Dark. Dark.
Dark. Dark. Dark.
Dark. Dark.
Dark.

It seemed to take years for the lift to reach bottom. But at the last the cage, with Boy cowering inside, came crashing to a stop.

Boy opened the iron door and stepped gingerly off the platform. Peering into the lightless depths, he staggered down the shaft.

The darkness
was the darkness
of the void
before Creation. There was no wind
blowing nowhere and the air was rank with
coal damp. The souls of long-dead miners shone like membranes in the no-light. The earth was groaning softly like an old drunk asleep in a gutter. Boy fumbled in the pockets of his jacket for a match.

A flickering. Torn shadows.

Hanging by a bent nail from the ceiling of the mineshaft, a trellis of ochred timbers unencumbered by cobwebs, was what looked like a rusty old kerosene lamp. The mantle was as dry as the bones of the pharoahs, but by using every match he had, Boy finally managed to coax it into flame. Holding the rusted lamp up like a beacon, he stared into the dark beyond its fragile sphere of light. The mineshaft seemed to angle to the left ever so slightly. There were beads of oily moisture on the black rock of the ceiling. Two narrow iron railway tracks, extravagantly corroded, were embedded in the avalanche of rubble on the floor.

So *this* is hell, Boy thought. Or heaven.

Or an old abandoned mineshaft in the hills above Nanaimo, in which, a million years ago, his father had once been a foreman, and into which the ratcatcher, Mr. Death, had disappeared.

And if Mr. Death had vanished down this mineshaft with his daughter, Boy decided, then somewhere, *somewhere*, in the tangled web of tunnels that extended in all directions through the raw stone of that mountain was the girl whom he had worshipped in his dreams ever since his childhood. Somewhere in that labyrinth was the object of his quest.

And so, having wandered through the tunnels of old No. 1 forever, stumbling over moraines or debris left behind by miners, skirting miles around cave-ins and pools of stagnant water, deafened by the rumbling of the mountain all around him, Boy found his way down to the ruins of the stables, where once that Yankee parson came to set his traps for rats.

As he stood there with his kerosene lamp in those old abandoned stables, Boy felt as if his destiny were finally complete. His father had built a labyrinth on the earth and there beneath it, and he had joined the two together with the thin thread of his life. There was nothing more to say or do. There was no need to go back to the surface. A blue-eyed girl sat waiting at the far end of the stables, her golden hair around her like a sea-wake of burning embers. Around her feet the blind rats seethed like waves around a piling.

Boy crashed his lamp against the wall and laughed into the void.

Calm Creek

Perhaps it was the sight of her, perched on the back of her pony at the shoreline, where the gangway ran down from the listing *Lady Mary*, with her parasol fluttering in the breeze from the ocean and her Negro porter stumbling in the sea-wash beside her, that made the photographer (whoever he may have been) decide, at that moment, to take a picture of her. Certainly she was beautiful, at 18 or 19, that summer of 1890. And there was nothing in her bearing to reveal what was to come.

But the photographer has apparently done something wrong with his camera, or there is simply too much light being reflected from the water. In any case, there it is, an enigmatic object: a girl, made of light, on an incandescent pony, with a small figure carved out of air by her side. The child (for she was holding her infant son, named Francis for his father) has been utterly lost in a torrent of light.

She is wearing the white dress that she bought in San Francisco, and the last of the several pairs of white lace gloves she bought for the voyage. Her dark hair uncoils on her delicate shoulders. She has come all the way from the state of California to be with her husband in this unknown, desolate place. It is the first time in her life that she has been without her family. Imagine how she feels inside, hovering at the shoreline.

The photograph was one of several James found in the drawer of an old oak dresser, the dresser in the corner of his grandmother's bedroom. Grandmother Rodgerson had passed away a few days earlier; and James had come home from the logging camp for the funeral, and to help his younger sisters take care of their mother, who had exhausted herself with the arrangements for the funeral, and had taken to her bed.

The woman in the picture was his grandmother's aunt by marriage, or a cousin of his grandmother's aunt, or something of that sort. Grandmother Rodgerson had mentioned her from time to time, not often. After all, she was a relative, if a distant one at best.

So James had heard the story of this woman several times, and remembered it that winter morning, chancing on her picture, as he stood there in the stillness of his grandmother's silent room.

The woman was the daughter of a California banker. She had married young, at 17, which was common enough in those days. Her husband was an engineer; his family had come from Scotland. He had invested all his money in a plan to mine for copper. When the first returns from the mine were poor, he had come up from California to take charge of the mine himself. He was twenty-five or thirty, not much older than his bride.

The mine was in the mountains at the head of MacKinley Inlet. A stream flowed down the mountainside from the slopes above the mine-site. It meandered down to the inlet, held in still pools on the ridges like the pearls on a woman's necklace. The miners called it Calm Creek. At the far end of the inlet was the village where James was born.

The man had left his teen-aged bride behind in California. He had set out for the mine in March; she gave birth to his child at the end of April. The summer passed, the autumn. All winter the girl heard nothing from the man who was her husband. When April came again, she made up her mind to travel north. The engineer had vanished into the mountains above the inlet. Inquiries at the postmaster's office in James' village had done no good.

Against her father's wishes, she booked passage on a schooner. The *Lady Mary* brought her north. She arrived in

James' village in the early part of May. And was captured in the lost light of that luminescent picture. And rode up through the village on her white-and-dappled pony, with her Negro porter slogging through the unfamiliar mud.

And vanished into memory. And was never seen again.

It was said her father came from Sacramento to try to find her. It was said her husband's mine had failed; that he had killed himself, his wife, his child. That her husband's mine had caved in, and she had arrived too late to save him. The woods around the inlet hold their secrets, some forever. In any case, she disappeared up the trail beside the inlet, and followed it where Calm Creek wove its webs along the ridges. Imagine how her white dress shone, by the pools of shady water. Imagine the dappled pony, stooped to drink from the lucent stream.

Calm Creek, Calm Creek.

*　*　*

When James left school he took a job with a man named Johnny Bolton. Bolton had a sawmill in the woods above the inlet. He worked it with his two sons, who were 22 and 20. His wife was cook and kept the accounts, and his daughter did the housework. When times were good, he hired a boy from the village to help out.

Alan Bolton, one of Johnny's sons, took James up to the sawmill. He had a boat, called *Calm Creek*, with a smoky Easthope motor. It was "clinker-built," he told James, and could withstand all but the roughest weather.

The two boys passed the voyage hardly speaking to each other. Alan Bolton, it seemed, was preoccupied, or taciturn by nature. And James was shy of talking to a boy a few years older than himself, a boy who worked and owned a boat and earned money for his father. James sat in the bow of the boat and watched his village slowly disappearing in the distance.

Alan Bolton's hawkish profile scanned the sunset on the water. The boat kicked up a rolling wake as it ploughed toward the sawmill. The narrow forms of cormorants dove serenely toward their shadows. It was almost dark by the time they reached the pier beside the mill.

All that summer, James stacked lumber from the ripsaw in the sawmill. The mill was built on a platform of timbers that rested on pilings driven deep into the creekbed, so that it stretched out nearly halfway over Calm Creek like a dock. The Bolton's house was nestled in the hillside just above it, far enough away from the mill for the scrawny pines that grew on the hill to dampen the sound of the ripsaw, but near enough for the men to have their lunch in the house. Sheltered from the landward breeze and the ubiquitous mosquitoes, they would sit on the screened verandah while Mrs. Bolton and the daughter brought them sandwiches and lemonade and a pot of coffee for Mr. Bolton. Exhausted from the morning's work, James and the Bolton boys would sprawl out in their chairs, savouring the sweet bite of the homemade lemonade. The elder brother, Arthur, was clever with his hands and had built feeders to attract the hummingbirds and hung them all around the verandah. On summer days, a dozen or so of the tiny birds would come to drink the sugared water from the tubes, thrumming at the flyscreen with their iridescent wings as the Bolton family sat inside and watched them.

Johnny Bolton had come out to the village from England in 1906 or '07 on a sailing ship much like the one in which the woman in the photograph had come up the coast from San Francisco. He had started out as a "hand-logger," cutting huge logs fifteen feet across from the heart of the virgin forest. In those days they used a two-man handsaw, a "Swede-fiddle" as they called it. They would notch the tree on both sides, then drive short planks into the notches. A man would stand on each of these planks, with the "Swede-fiddle" stretched out between them. By heaving the handsaw back and forth, they would laboriously cut down the tree.

"Those old Swede-fiddles weren't as bad as you'd think,"

he confided to James one evening. "As long as you had another fellow with you, you could cut down a tree with no trouble. It was when you had to use one of the buggers alone that it could get to be a bit of a problem. You wasted so much time running back and forth from one handle to the other, you'd be lucky not to miss your dinner before you finally got the damn tree down."

He had a teasing sense of humour, like the humour of the Indians with whom he had worked when he was a logger. He had long since tried out all of his tall tales on his family, and James provided him with an audience that hadn't heard it all before. His favourite stories concerned the mythical beasts that inhabit the world of the logger, and he was always looking for ways to introduce them unobtrusively into the conversation, hoping to string his listener along for as long as he could.

"Pinnacle grouse," he would mutter, cocking his head to one side like a hunting dog to listen to the faint squawk of birds in the pine trees around the verandah.

Try as he might to resist the temptation, James' curiosity would invariably overwhelm him, and he would have to break down and ask Bolton what a "pinnacle grouse" might be.

"Never heard of a pinnacle grouse, Jimmy?" Bolton would ask him, shaking his head in amazement. "Don't your teachers tell you anything? I wonder why they pay them. Might as well live on some other planet as go to school in that village of yours."

He would pause for a moment to light his pipe, and then, squinting up into the windblown pines with a look of hard-won wisdom, begin to tell his tale.

"A pinnacle grouse is a bird with just one wing, so it can fly around the pinnacle of some mountain. They even lay eggs that are square, like dice, so the damn things won't roll down the slopes."

James enjoyed Johnny Bolton's family as he had never enjoyed his own. The two boys, Alan and Arthur, were both quiet and uncomplaining. They both worked long hours at the mill six days a week, and they spent their Sundays listening to cowboy songs on the radio, building model airplanes, or working on their cars. The yard was full of car parts and bits of engines under canvas tarps, and it wasn't uncommon to find a bowl of piston-rings soaking in solvent on the dresser in their bedroom, or a row a gleaming wing-nuts perched like cabbage whites on their desk. Both of the boys had girlfriends who were nurses down the coast, and they would hitch a ride to Vancouver on the mailboat every second weekend, returning home late Sunday night with a tin of Player's Navy Cut tobacco for their dad and some chocolates for their mother and their sisters. Mrs. Bolton was an Irishwoman, and her maiden name was Reilly, but she had none of the Irish gaiety or temper. It was in her daughter Elsie that the Irish had come out. Her hair was burnished copper and her eyes were green as jade, and she seemed to like nothing better than stirring up a commotion. She had her father's teasing humour, and it was perhaps because she so obviously took after him in this respect that he could never bring himself to reprimand her, even when she teased her poor mother nearly out of her wits. Hardly a day would go by without her announcing without a hint of a smile that the potroast her mother had been cooking had been burnt to a lump of charcoal, or that she had decided to chop all her hair off and join a convent in Quebec.

James had little experience with girls, and he had never met anyone remotely like Elsie Bolton. She was 16 years old that summer, almost two years younger than he was, but whenever he was with her he felt immature and ungainly, like an unco-ordinated puppy that can't walk without tripping over its paws. She had been to Vancouver and Toronto, places James had only heard of, and lived at a fancy boarding school in Victoria during the winters. Having grown up in that isolated house with her father and her older brothers, she was completely at ease in the company of men, and treated James as if he were one of the family.

If Elsie found life at Calm Creek boring after her winters at the girls' school, she certainly never showed it. She would be up not long after six every morning, and would come out to the sleeping porch where James and Alan Bolton slept with a cup of coffee for each of them before seven. By seven-thirty, she would have the breakfast served, and be helping her mother with the housework. On Sundays, she would take a pail and go blackberrying in the hills above Calm Creek. There were several abandoned farms in those hills, where settlers had tried to make a go of it and failed in the early days before the turn of the century. The bush had been slowly reclaiming the farms, and the split-rail fences and cedar-shake barns were covered with tangles of blackberry vines that could be reached without using a ladder. As no one else picked them but Elsie, the vines were always loaded with berries, and she could easily gather enough to fill her bucket in less than an hour.

It was Elsie's mother who suggested that she take James along on one of her expeditions up to the berrying fields. It was a hot July Sunday, and the Bolton boys had gone to see their girlfriends down the coast. James was sitting on the verandah with one of Arthur's Zane Grey westerns, but he didn't feel like reading on such a lovely summer morning, and he had rested the open pocketbook on the arm of his chair and was gazing through the flyscreen at the trees beside the mill, where the river waters glimmered through the pine boughs.

"Take Jimmy with you, Else," James heard Mrs. Bolton say. "He's at a loose end with your brothers gone, and the two of you can gather enough berries for some pies. I want to invite Mrs. Rushford here next weekend."

Elsie's reply was lost among the squawking of the crows, but in a moment she came out onto the verandah with her pail. She sat down on the canopied swing and cuddled the pail in her lap.

"You've been drafted, my lad," she said. "And it won't do

you any good to resist. Mother says you're helping me pick berries this afternoon, so you might as well put away your book and come along without a struggle. Think of it as service to the Empire, or something like that. I should think you'll get the Victoria Cross, if you promise to carry the pails. And she's packing some turkey sandwiches, so we won't have to live on red ants. Are you any good at wrestling with cougars?"

"Not much, I'm afraid," James said. He picked up the book and marked his place. "I'll see if I can find some better shoes." He looked at his feet. "I'm afraid I've ruined these working in the sawmill."

He stood up and walked to the door to the livingroom, leaving Elsie smiling coyly to herself.

"You needn't worry about shoes," she said. "I haven't booked an orchestra. There won't be time to dance. Just see if you can find a bucket in the toolshed."

James blushed and retreated into the cool of the house. Every time he talked to Elsie, he came away feeling foolish. He knew that he was painfully shy, especially where girls were concerned, but most of the girls he'd known at school were almost as shy as he was, and they never made him feel so gauche and awkward. Yet Elsie made the other girls he knew seem dull and insubstantial, and he was glad that he had been given the chance to spend a few hours alone with her. He smiled to Mrs. Bolton, who was packing a picnic lunch for them in the kitchen, and walked through the house to the sleeping porch to look for a better pair of shoes.

The trail along the southern bank of Calm Creek was level and quite well-trodden, but it still took almost an hour for James and Elsie to reach even the most accessible of the abandoned farms. Although little else remained of the fence around the hayfield, the gate was still standing: a stout, cross-barred structure of weathered grey timbers that hung between two heavy posts made of squared-off cedar logs. The sight of this gate standing all by itself seemed comical, almost dreamlike. James ran ahead into the sunlight with a suitable flourish, so that Elsie could walk through it into the field. But of course the hinges were seized with rust, and the gate, for all his tugging, clung stubbornly to its posts.

"Careful, you'll let the ghosts out," Elsie laughed. She pretended to step over the non-existent fence, and then walked off toward the swaybacked barn at the edge of the field. The barn and the farmhouse beside it had been weathered to the colour of granite. The roofs were full of ragged holes where high winds had torn off the shingles. Blackberry vines had imposed themselves through the gaps in the leeched grey wood.

"I wonder who lived here," James said, peering through the doorways into empty, mildewed rooms.

"Finns, or so my father says," Elsie answered, handing James her bucket while she clambered up onto a windowsill so that she could reach the most succulent, sun-ripened berries.

"Finns? You mean people from Finland?"

"Finns, Swedes, Skywegians, something like that. Most of this land was cleared and farmed by people from that part of the world. It reminded them of Scandinavia, I suppose, with all the fjords and mountains."

"Why do you think they abandoned this place? Did they just get sick of farming? Or did they all die off or something?"

"I expect they would have died by now, all right. We all do eventually, or hadn't you heard? They probably just found that it was easier to make a living fishing or logging. It couldn't have been very much fun, you know, trying to make a go of it on a little farm like this."

James worked his way slowly along the side of the old house, picking berries from the tangles of vines and dropping them into his bucket. The abandoned farmhouse haunted him, filled his mind with unanswerable questions. He wondered if someone would chance on his own village someday while exploring in the woods above the inlet, and find that there was nothing left but a clutch of derelict houses with the glass in all the windows shattered and weeds growing up through the floors.

"You're looking very pensive," Elsie said. She hopped down from the windowsill. "I've already filled my bucket. Do you think it's too early to start eating lunch? I could absolutely murder a sandwich."

Her teeth were stained purple from eating the berries. When she saw that James had noticed this, she stuck out her tongue, which was also purple. Laughing, she retrieved the picnic basket from the long grass beside the farmhouse. She unfolded the red-checked tablecloth that was lying on top of the basket and spread it out in the shade of a leafy maple.

"Hurry up if you don't want to starve to death," she said. "I'll have eaten it all in a minute." She began to unpack the sandwiches and the thermos flask from the basket. "Mother really seems to have outdone herself; there's even a little pot of cranberry sauce, and a jar of her homemade pickles. I can see that I'm going to have to bring you along more often; she usually gives me a crust of dry bread and any leftover gruel that the dog has rejected. I suppose she doesn't want you telling the village how she neglects her only daughter. I hope the lemonade is sweet enough; the last time I had a glass of it I couldn't whistle for a week."

James put down his bucket and sprawled out on the grass beside her. The matted grass was soft and warm, and the light that filtered down through the translucent leaves of the maple cast variegated shadows on the brilliant checkered cloth. The silence was absolute but for the chirping of the crickets, and the field of burned-off grass seemed suffused with golden light.

"Wouldn't you like to own this place?" James asked. "And to live here, with all your family?"

"Oh, of course I would," Elsie answered. She balanced her cup of lemonade on a mound beside the tablecloth and reached for another sandwich. "How could anything be more wonderful than to live in this rotten old farmhouse, with hot and cold running field mice and the rain pouring in through the hole in the roof and a friendly cougar for your next-door neighbour! You could probably shoot your own breakfast without getting out of bed in the morning, and the flies and wasps and wood lice and things would do a lovely job of cleaning up the scraps!"

"That's not what I meant," James muttered. He flushed and turned away from Elsie. For a moment they both sat in silence, neither knowing how to bridge the rift that had opened up between them. A tarnished silver thread of cloud uncoiled across the mountains. In the distance, dark birds chattered through the thin boughs of the pines.

"I know that's not what you meant," Elsie said. "I don't know why I have to be so sarcastic." She stood up and began to brush the dried bits of grass from her skirt and the sleeves of her sweater. "Old Miss Hotchkiss at St. Margaret's says I have a tongue like a piece of barbed wire. I don't know why people put up with me; I'm such a thoughtless bitch sometimes."

She knelt and began to pack the lunch things back into the basket.

"It doesn't matter," James said. He stood up and reached for the two pails of berries. "We'd better start back, I suppose. Your mother will be wondering what's become of us."

"Yes, I suppose we'd better get these berries home quickly so she can bake her precious pies. There's some old dragon from her church group coming over on the weekend, or so I hear. I suppose she needs the pastry for burnt offerings."

She folded up the tablecloth and arranged it on top of the basket. The patchwork of soft light that filtered through the branches burned gold in her hair as she knelt in the long grass and fussed with the cloth. James stood there and clutched the wire loops of the heavy pails in his hands, silenced by the whiteness of her pale throat in the sunlight, the curve of her breasts against her plain white cotton blouse, the grace of her delicate shoulders. When she stood up, her green eyes met his for an instant, and then she was past him and away across the

94

hayfield, swinging the basket with its red-checkered cloth by her side, her auburn hair gleaming in the sunlight.

James watched her disappearing through the bare fields for a moment, then lifted the pails and followed her toward the abandoned gate. The tendrils of the windblown clouds flowed slowly across the sun. There was no sound but the murmuring of Calm Creek.

*　　*　　*

The memory flowed and shimmered like a reflection on a stream. James gently returned the photograph to its place between the pages of his grandmother's well-worn Bible, then closed the book and put it back in the drawer of the dresser. He ran his fingers absentmindedly across the smooth wood of the dresser, on which were arranged his grandmother's things: her silver-backed hairbrush, some tortoise-shell combs, the cameo brooch she had worn out from England. These objects seemed forlorn to James, deprived of their purpose and meaning. He picked up a delicate hand-mirror with a pattern of flowers on its handle, remembering how, as a child, he had liked to sneak into his grandmother's room and hold that little hand-mirror up to the large oval mirror on the back of her dresser, so that the two mirrors reflected each other, forming an infinite tunnel of light. He would imagine that these reflections were a doorway, a passage that would lead him to unimaginable worlds. Remembering this, James held up his grandmother's mirror to the larger one on the dresser; but the shimmering infinity of mirrors held no magic, and there was no door that would lead him from his grandmother's empty room.

That summer, fifteen years ago, was the last time James had seen Elsie Bolton. She had graduated from her girls' school in Victoria the following year, gone east to college, married. Her brothers had gone into business; they were both living in Vancouver. Their father, Johnny Bolton, sold the sawmill when the two boys left. There was nothing in it for him with his children gone, he told James. He retired and went to join them in Vancouver.

The man who bought the sawmill burned it down a few years later. He had tried to make a go of it, but the big concerns from back east and the States were slowly squeezing out the little independent mills, and eventually he could no longer sell enough of his rough-cut planks to make a living and keep going. When the mill burned down, it was obvious to everyone in the village that he'd set the fire himself, and the insurance men refused to pay him for the damage. He sold the gang-saws off for scrap and boarded up the house. There was nothing left but a wharf of blackened timbers over Calm Creek.

A few months after the mill burned down, Alan Bolton phoned James from Vancouver. Alan's father, it seemed, had gone back up to Calm Creek with the intention of rebuilding the mill. He had grown restive in retirement, predictably enough, and had apparently talked of nothing but his sawmill. He had hitched a ride on a fishing boat and gone back to the site of the mill, determined to have it running again by summer.

He was seventy now, and his heart was bad. He would kill himself rebuilding that sawmill.

At Alan's request, James borrowed a boat from a fisherman friend and set out for the old place on Calm Creek. When he got there, Johnny Bolton was perched on what was left of the timbers that had once supported the mill, trying to cut the charred wood from the top of a piling with a handsaw. There was nothing much left of the mill itself and the tool sheds that had once stood behind it, and the pilings and the timbers were as blackened as stumps in a slash fire. Securing the bowline of his boat to a piling, James clambered up the wheelhouse and onto the wharf, then worked his way carefully to where Johnny was squatting, rasping ineffectually away at the wood with his saw.

"Had a phone call from Alan this morning," James said.

The old man looked up without recognition at James for a moment, then went back to his sawing as if no one were there.

"He's concerned that you're biting off more than you can chew with this business," James continued. "Times aren't what they were in the woods now; you know that. Let's round up your gear and I'll take you back home."

The old man stopped sawing and gestured shakily around him at what had once been his sawmill.

"Young Alan didn't build this, goddamn it," he whispered. "I cut these damn timbers with my own hands thirty years back. I built the damn house and I ran the damn sawmill. There was never any problem. People always need wood."

He turned his back on James and resumed his futile labour. James repeated what Alan had told him, but the old man was deaf to persuasion. He set his mouth in a firm, determined line and sawed frantically away at the wharf. Unsure of what he should do with the old man, James left him sawing at his perch on the wharf and made his way up the trail from the sawmill. It saddened him to see the old house with its windows boarded up, and yet the sight of the screened verandah and the raucous squawking of the crows in the pines brought back thoughts of that long-vanished summer. He remembered old Johnny's fanciful tales of the pinnacle grouse and the sidehill gouger. How many times had he retold those tales to the children of his friends and neighbours, appropriating not only the substance of the tale, but also Johnny's deadpan delivery and gentle, teasing humour?

Unfastening the rusted hook-and-eye latch from the door of the screened verandah, James mounted the wooden steps and walked over to the remains of the canopied swing where Elsie Bolton had sat and laughed at his clumsiness one hot July morning a lifetime before. The swing had lost its canopy, and the chains from which it hung had rusted solid, but the wooden seat seemed firm enough, and supported James' weight when he sat down. Far below, he could make out the shape of the wharf and the hunched form of old Johnny Bolton; in the distance the waters of the inlet lay gleaming, tinted violet and blue by the cool autumn sunset.

I have lived all my life in this place, James thought. But the words had no meaning, captured nothing of the lost dreams and luminous memories that flowed past his mind's eye like high cirrus clouds on a cool autumn day. He sat in the old swing and gazed through the rusted remains of the flyscreen at the waters that endlessly flowed down from Calm Creek, endlessly losing themselves in the sea.

*　　*　　*

Once, when James was working at a logging camp fifty miles or so north of the village, he hitched a ride south with an Indian fisherman to visit his mother while he had a few days off. It was early in spring, and the fog had rolled in; but the skipper, Walter Amos, was an old west coast hand and could negotiate the gaps between the razor-backed islands and submarine reefs that ranged out from the coast with the effortless precision of a sleepwalker. James relaxed in the wheelhouse with a cup of hot tea while the blurred shapes of slate cliffs topped with gaunt, tortured pines drifted past through the haze as they chugged down the coastline.

Walter Amos had brought his wife along to visit relatives in the south. She was a Haida girl from Skidegate, and had the pale skin and coppery hair which, through some quirk of heredity, appear in some Haida women. She was shy of James, naturally enough, and would neither talk nor meet his eyes. She passed the time cooing stories to her sleeping infant son, in a transparent attempt to avoid making conversation. James recognized the stories the woman whispered to her child; they were versions of the folktales of the Haida. James smiled to himself as she recounted the exploits of the crow who stole the sun, the boy made of pitch, and the skin-shifting woman.

There was a certain tale, however, that James had never heard before. It concerned a pale-skinned woman who had wandered into the woods. Her hair was burnished copper and her eyes as green as glass. Her skin was the pearly silver of a seashell. She was looking for her husband, who was hunting in the hills. There was no one in her village who would look after her infant son, so she had wrapped him in a woven shawl and brought him with her to the woods. There was no sign of her husband. He seemed to have vanished from the earth. With every step the woman took, she became more lost and confused. The trees and rocks around her seemed to melt and change their shapes. Birds, or ghosts, called out her name as she walked among the trees. Every moment took her farther from her village. At last she came to a shining stream, and sat down on its bank to rest. She was tired, and soon she fell asleep, her child curled to her breast. As they slept, the spirits turned them into herons.

James sat back and sipped his tea as Walter Amos' wife told her tale. Certainly the story brought to mind his grandmother's aunt, and he saw again her photograph dissolving into light, and remembered her ill-starred journey to the heartland. And certainly other images from the past flowed through his mind: graceful birds with ice-white wings that flew beyond the sun; Elsie Bolton with her auburn hair and moods like summer storms; old Johnny spinning tales on his verandah.

But what remained in his mind the longest was the image of that stream, an image that was neither time nor memory nor his life, but was only water shining as it shimmered over stones, the gentle waters flowing down from Calm Creek.

Another Sad Day
at the Edge of the Empire

Doctor Grimaldi was lying in a hammock on the crumbling verandah of his rotting Georgian mansion on the hill above the village sipping whiskey from a jam jar, utterly oblivious to everything around him, from the mewling of the seagulls as they soared up from the harbour to the clatter of the rain that had been falling since the first day of Creation on the roof of the verandah, when his crazy wife Amelie, who had spent the morning sitting in her bath composing sonnets while pretending she was posing for the painter Botticelli, came flouncing through the doorway with a look of pure despair.

"God has given up on us all," she announced, sniffing at the withered gardenias in the planter and favouring her husband with an enigmatic smile.

It was all that Grimaldi could do to keep himself from visibly wincing when he heard his wife's ridiculous remark. Her obsession with the spiritual was killing him. While he had raised no objection to her cluttering up the homestead with a veritable boatload of mystical claptrap, Tarot cards and crystal balls and Ouija boards and so forth, and had even kept his mouth shut when she started getting friendly with the rest of the local Cassandras, a motley collection of hysterical spinsters who were constantly fluttering about in the parlour, muttering portents and swilling his liquor, these gnomic pronouncements were more than he could bear. It was like living with the Cumaean Sybil.

"What the devil are you on about, Amelie?" he asked her, drooling a mouthful of whiskey down his shirt front. "Why would someone like God give a damn about us?"

But there was no use in trying to humour her. The woman had an answer for everything. With the faultless, if circular, logic of childhood, she fixed her doe's eyes on him and parried his question, pursing her lips in a little crimson pout.

"Because He told me when I asked Him, that's why."

"For Christ's sake, Amelie, He doesn't just go around yapping at people." Grimaldi sighed, exhausted with the effort of carrying on an argument which he knew, from experience, to be utterly futile. "Anyway, God wouldn't be caught dead in a hick town like this one," he added. "For one thing, he couldn't stand this everlasting rain."

"All right for you, then," Amelie replied, as she vanished like a shadow through the doorway to the parlour, her tattered emerald ballgown raising dust clouds from the carpets, which hadn't been beaten since the previous autumn, when the maid had gotten plastered on Grimaldi's home-made whiskey and drowned herself out in the birdbath in the yard. "But something dreadful is going to happen; I can feel it in the wind."

God damn her, Grimaldi thought, gazing at his shattered reflection in the jam jar; what the hell's the use of talking to her, anyway? He might just as well go yammer at the breadbox in the kitchen, for all the good it did him to waste his time with her. Translucent as a spirit, knowing neither rhyme nor reason, she wandered through the variegated shadows of his life.

The bell tower in the village, which was somewhere down below him through the twisted strands of jack pine, dolefully tolled out the twelve strokes of noon. Pitching his jam jar off the side of the verandah and clambering out of the folds of the hammock, Doctor Grimaldi got ready for work. That was one thing, he thought, about having your practice in this godforsaken village in the middle of nowhere: at least you didn't have to be sober to perform. After fumbling about with his monogrammed cufflinks, carved from the shell of a single abalone, and straightening the knot on the gaudy silk tie with the map of Madagascar that Amelie had found him in the Salvation Army, he staggered through the parlour and whistled for his dogs. In a moment the pair of them, lanky yellow cougar hounds, materialized beside him, issuing from the umberous darkness of the kitchen, where they liked to sprawl out on the rug by the stove. As he ventured through the French doors into the greyness of the rainstorm, unfurling his umbrella like some mediaeval weapon, the two dogs loped behind him, nuzzling at his heels. The rattle of their blunt claws on the sidewalk was a comfort.

Rain, rain, and more bloody rain, Grimaldi thought, turning up the collar of his coat against the deluge. The damn stuff had been falling for so long that he couldn't remember what the world looked like without it. They might just as well be living at the bottom of the sea. Striding past the wreckage of his crumpled black DeSoto, which had languished in the driveway since the previous October, its engine rusted solid and its windows furred with mildew, he gathered his black leather bag to his body and stumbled down the pathway to the village far below.

It was then that he noticed that the tide was going out. In fact, it had already gone out so far that the fishing boats moored at the wharves in the harbour were lying on their sides like a beached school of dolphins washed up in the wake of some tropical hurricane, while the harbour itself was a long gleaming desert, as grey as polished onyx, festooned with scraps of fishing nets and gleaming clumps of stone. In all of the years that he had lived in that village, clinging like a mollusc to the rim of the Pacific, Grimaldi had never seen anything like this. It must, he decided, be the result of some unusual natural phenomenon, like sunspots or gamma rays or lunar occlusions, or whatever it was that the scientists called them, that was causing the sea to go that far from the shore.

Anyway, he thought, as he fished in his pockets for his silver cigarette case, cursing the wind as it whipped at his umbrella, there had to be a rational explanation. It wasn't, after all, as if the sea was just something that you could turn on and off whenever the spirit moved you, like that fancy electric toaster that he'd bought for Amelie, in which the dizzy broad had tried to fry the neighbours' cat. Nosirree Bob, he muttered, striking a match on the shaft of his umbrella and shielding the flame from the wind with the matchbook, an old trick he'd learned from his days in the Navy, once you had yourself an ocean it was there for the duration, right smack dab where you had found it in the first place, allowing a little for the winds and tides and so forth. It was something you could count on, like the Anglican church.

But by the time that Grimaldi had picked his way down through the patches of stinkweed and the malevolent nettles that were gradually obscuring the pathway to his office, it was obvious, even to someone who hadn't been sober for two days together since the still had exploded in the middle of a seance the previous winter, that something out of the ordinary had happened in the town. The bedraggled Red Ensign that the village magistrate, postmaster, building inspector, notary and all-purpose civil servant, Old Angus MacKenzie, had been running up the flagpole in front of the courthouse every morning since the Bronze Age, had been removed and replaced with a torn swath of sailcloth, in the centre of which was a daub of red paint. And the town clock was bonging its brains out again, although it couldn't have been more than twenty minutes since the last time Grimaldi had heard it, and the worthless thing was only supposed to chime once an hour. On the twelfth ring Grimaldi furled up his umbrella and, using it to beat back the stubborn clumps of thistles, quickened his pace in the direction of his office. By the time it reached fifteen, he was already in town.

The streets of the village were utterly deserted. There was absolutely no one in the shops or on the sidewalks. There were no cars on the empty streets, no faces in the windows. Televisions nattered to themselves in empty houses. It was as if the entire populace had been swept out with the tide.

Everyone must have gone down to the harbour, Grimaldi decided, whistling to his hound-dogs as they trotted through the quagmire. The village was made up of weathered fishing shanties, each one of which leaned hopefully toward its nearest neighbour, as if only the strength of numbers could withstand the demonic rainstorms. There had been times in the past, as the doctor could remember, when it had seemed as if the whole town would be torn up from its moorings and blown clear across the Pacific, so that they would go to bed in British Columbia and wake up in the middle of the China Sea. But today there was only the implacable rainfall, which was so much a part of Grimaldi's life, and everyone's, that it hardly seemed to matter. And it seemed as if the ocean itself, instead of them, had blown away.

By the time the doctor arrived at the door of his office, he was very nearly sober, and soaked to the skin. Extracting his latchkey from its nest behind the mailbox, he wrestled with the rusty old lock for a moment, then finally managed to make his way inside. Having gained the haven of that stuffy little office, which was really no more than a tarpapered shack perched on stilts above the harbour with a gangway to connect it to the main street of the village and a shingle by the doorway that displayed his name in Gothic letters, Doctor Grimaldi breathed a sigh of relief. With Amelie and her cronies in his mansion on the hillside, leafing through their *grimoires* and reciting incantations, his office had become a sort of home away from home. After sloughing off his raincoat and hanging his umbrella on the gilt frame of the portrait of the Old Queen and her consort, both mugging for the camera like a pair of withered gargoyles, that hung above his oak desk with its scroll legs and its blotter, Grimaldi took a test tube from the rack beside the windows, wiped it with his shirt-tail, and poured himself a drink.

This was the time of the day that he liked best. Standing in the middle of that cosy, cluttered office with his test tube full of whiskey and his dogs curled up on the doormat at his feet, surrounded by the sanctified relics of his profession, from the forceps sprawled open on the stained and mildewed counter to the box of mouldy cotton swabs and the ancient, rust-flecked scalpel, gave the doctor a feeling of good will toward men. If only, he reflected, he could remain that way forever, alone in the midst of his own little kingdom, that tranquil world illumined by the flawless light of Science, with its jars of pickled foetuses and its vials with strange inscriptions that gleamed like holy ikons on the dust-covered shelves around him, he would never have to worry about anything on earth.

But already, as he stood there, he could smell the scent of jasmine that was wafting down the staircase from the bedroom in the attic, where his mistress, The Other Amelie, was lying in the brass bed he had brought her back from England, dreaming of the snowfields of the distant Himalayas and purring like a lioness in the violet light of candles, with her auburn hair unravelled on the bedsheets all around her, burning through the shadows like a thousand tongues of flame. Swilling down the last dregs of his putrid homemade whiskey and inserting the empty test tube in the ribcage of the skeleton that was hanging from the ceiling in the corner of the office with a sausage in its pelvis and a rose between its teeth, Grimaldi staggered over to the bottom of the staircase and, inhaling gusts of jasmine air and puffing like a grampus, ascended through the darkness to the tiny room above.

The Other Amelie was lying on her stomach in the middle of the brass bed, with her golden breasts pressed flat against the jasmine-scented bedspread and the light like molten lava in the hollow of her spine. There was a volume of DeQuincey lying open at her elbow, although the doctor had long suspected that she couldn't read or write. The room was lined with tapestries of sacred birds and centaurs, salvaged from the wreckage of a rusty Hong Kong trader that had foundered in the harbour on the night of the eclipse. For some reason or other, the sight of these exotic creatures, emblazoned in golden filagree and beaming down like blind gods on the useless, precious objects that the woman had collected from the four points of the compass, from monkeys stuffed with pampas grass to Roc's eggs from Sumatra, oppressed the doctor's senses as he sat down on the bed.

"If this infernal rain doesn't stop before long," he muttered as he shrugged off his suspenders, "I think I'll go back home and cut my throat."

The sound of his voice woke The Other Amelie. As he tugged off his trousers and stretched out beside her, she lazily propped herself up on one elbow and watched him, drinking in his presence with her whiskey-coloured eyes. Although it seemed so long ago, the doctor could still remember the first day that he'd found her, sitting in the eternal downpour on the gangway to his office, surrounded by the flotsam of her pitiful possessions, her ornate wicker cages full of birds of every species, her conch shells filled with polished stones, her strings of Spanish onions, an orphan of so many storms that she could map the whole Pacific in the moisture on a window and knew the names of all the winds and secret, cunning tides. The first thing he had noticed was her resemblance to his wife. It was as if the two women were sisters, or the separated halves of some hypothetical being, with Amelie embodying the ethereal aspects, her mind full of dark rooms and devious angles, and this other girl the more physical side, elemental as the sea.

Grimaldi couldn't live without either of the women. They seemed to correspond, somehow, to the two different sides of his being. Too much time with either of them would have driven him to distraction: sharing quarters with Amelie was like waltzing with a whirlwind—nothing was ever quite what it seemed to be, and what it seemed to be kept changing— while The Other Amelie seemed at times like an animated statue, a doll he had created out of bits of mud and straw. To cope with this dilemma, he had taken to partitioning his waking hours between the two Amelies, spending mornings, evenings, and every night in his mansion with the first Amelie, and lying in bed all afternoon with Amelie number two.

This scheme would have proven unworkable, of course, if the doctor had been busy with his practice. As it was, however, the arrival of a sick person at the doorway to his office was such an unusual occurrence that he had come to think of patients as semi-mythical beings, mentioned occasionally in medical journals but rarer in real life than unicorns or centaurs, and to assume that the diseases he'd learned about as a student were fictional creations or things of the past.

Not that the lack of paying customers made any difference to Grimaldi. Patients, in his experience, took all the fun out of being a doctor. They were constantly complaining about their tedious diseases, and they would get all hot under the collar if you did the least thing wrong. Oh, they were friendly enough as long as you were healing all their injuries and solving all their problems, but just amputate the wrong limb *once*, or do a little Caesarean section on someone who wasn't pregnant, and they'd treat you like a leper for the rest of your life. That was what was wrong with the world, Grimaldi decided, as he lay back and basked in the warmth of that bedroom with the moonshine whiskey coursing through his veins like a sirocco and The Other Amelie nuzzling like a lion cub at his shoulder: people could be so critical, so quick to take offence.

And besides, he reflected, he didn't really need his practice. Amelie had inherited enough money to keep the pair of them solvent for the forseeable future, and little villages in the middle of nowhere are economical places to live. There was absolutely nothing for him to worry about. He could lie right back and listen to the falling rain forever, and every day would trickle past just like the one before.

But then, just as he was about to doze off in the wide bed in that room above his office, his reverie was shattered by a voice from far below. It was, unmistakably, the voice of old man MacKenzie.

Outraged that anyone could be so inconsiderate as to disturb his meditations, Grimaldi leapt across the room and wrenched the window open. By kneeling on the windowsill and craning his neck in all directions, he managed to catch sight of his tormentor down below.

The magistrate, a distressingly fat man in an old-fashioned frock coat and brown leather gaiters, was pacing back and forth on the wet gravel slope beneath Grimaldi's upstairs window, where a good-sized piece of the Pacific ocean would normally have been. An apoplectic Scotsman who had emigrated from the slums of Glasgow, he had idled away the war years as the local commander of the Pacific Coast Militia, an ill-assorted collection of octogenarian Swedish fishermen and tongue-tied Indian trappers, anyone too old or sick to be off in Europe fighting, whose job it was to skulk around the inlets near the village, keeping a weather eye out for the invading Japanese. Not one to take such a sacred trust lightly, MacKenzie was still convinced, over thirty years later, that the slant-eyed yellow demons were still hiding out there somewhere, lying on the bottom in their camouflaged submarines, playing it cosy and biding their time. Any day now, he would tell you, they'd sneak ashore and overwhelm the villagers, ravishing their womenfolk and committing hari-kari all over their lawns.

When he saw the doctor leaning drunkenly from the upstairs window, MacKenzie waved a chubby fist in the direction of the ocean, which had dwindled away to a misty arc of colourless light at the edge of the distant horizon.

"It's those damn Japs," he bellowed, peering up at Grimaldi. "The bastards have turned off the Japanese current."

"What the hell are you on about, you silly old bugger?" Grimaldi asked, scratching pensively at his buttocks. "Has something really gone wrong down there, or have you just been putting too much gin in your camomile tea?"

"Has something gone wrong?" the older man shrieked, hopping frantically around on the gravel. "What in the name of all that's holy does it look like, you pill-pushing cretin? The whole bloody ocean has up and absconded! We'll be living in the middle of the prairies if this keeps up!"

"Oh, don't be so ridiculous. An ocean can't just vanish. Even a brainless old Presbyterian like you should know a simple thing like that."

"Then where the hell is all the water?" the Scotsman screamed, practically choking on his fury.

"Oh, I see now; it's water you want. Why didn't you say

so?" Grimaldi muttered, leaning farther out the window. By the time he'd finished relieving himself down the side of the weatherbeaten building, the magistrate had clambered up the slope and disappeared.

The Scotsman, as it turned out, wasn't the only one who had vanished. When Grimaldi slammed the window shut and staggered back across the bedroom, tacking like a storm-wracked sloop in the general direction of The Other Amelie's big brass four-poster, he discovered to his consternation that she was no longer lying in the bed. Nor, for that matter, was she anywhere else in the bedroom.

Now where on earth could she have gone? Grimaldi wondered. Reasoning that she could have slipped downstairs to get something from his office, he steadied himself as best he could and lurched toward the stairs. As he cautiously traversed the patchwork of bamboo mats and threadbare Afghan carpets with which the woman had covered the floor of her bedroom, he could see himself reflected from a dozen different angles, mirrored in the gold glass eyes of lemurs, owls, and falcons, hovering in silver bowls and cups of burnished copper, as if each of The Other Amelie's exotic playthings had some-how, while his back was turned, conspired to steal his soul. For one vertiginous moment he could feel himself dissolving, as if the transitory images reflected in every shiny surface in the room were more real than he was, than he could ever hope to be. Conscious of his nakedness, he sat down on the edge of the bed and pulled on his trousers, fumbling with the buttons as if his fingers were made of wax. By the time he had succeeded in tugging his shirt on and looping some semblance of a knot into his necktie, his mouth felt like one of those scalding red patches on a wall map of Asia Minor, signifying places where it only rains once every thirty or forty years. Getting dressed was no business for the faint of heart, he decided: Houdini himself would have blanched at the task.

"*Amelie?*" he whispered as he stumbled down the staircase. There was no reply to his quavering call, however: the girl had left the building, left the village, left the world. His office, when he reached it, was a frozen block of silence, empty except for his cougar hounds, still curled up in a tangle of muzzles and paws on the carpet, and his old friend the skeleton, which seemed to be shivering in the draft from the windows, its toothy grin clenched on the stem of its rose. On the shelves beside the windows, the foetuses sparkled like watery opals. The scalpel winked knowingly from its nest among the Q-Tips. Queen Vicky and Prince Albert glared contemptuously from the portrait. Every object in that office seemed to share some unspeakable secret. It was obviously, Grimaldi realized, well past time for another drink.

But when he delved into the bowels of his crinkled black doctor's bag, prizing forth his whiskey jug as if he were delivering some drunkard's baby, he discovered to his horror that the blasted thing was empty. Frantic, he ransacked every cupboard in the office, throwing mildewed files and rolls of gauze over his shoulders like confetti. Could he possibly have been foolish enough not to have provided himself with an extra bottle? The spectre of cold sobriety rose above him like the ghost of Christmas Future. If only he had had the foresight to provide for times like these!

There was, however, if memory served, a drop or two up in his mansion. Reluctant as he naturally was to desert his sacred calling in the middle of a workday, there was simply nothing for it but to scoot back up the hill. Untangling his umbrella from the portrait of Their Brittanic What's-its, he whistled his slumbering hounds awake and stumbled out the door.

Accustomed as he was to drinking gallons of that noxious homemade white lightning, a single teaspoon of which would have reduced a lesser mortal to drooling incoherence, it was a measure of Grimaldi's inebriation on this particular occasion that he was halfway up the hill before he noticed that the rain had stopped. There he was attempting to extricate himself from the tangles of homicidal blackberry vines which had draped themselves seductively from one side of the pathway to the other, when the sunlight that had already burned off the clouds found its way through the haze in his brain.

The lack of inclement weather hit the doctor like a bolt of lightning. Screwing up his eyes against the unfamiliar sunlight, he paused in a thicket of nettles and squinted myopically at the dazzling landscape, which seemed to have suddenly leapt into focus, as though a layer of gauze had been removed from his eyes. Far below him, by the harbour, he could see the village houses gleaming whitely in the sunshine, their cedar shingles steaming in the warmth of the midsummer sun. The harbour, stripped of its ocean, looked as dry as the Kalahari desert. Solar winds blew dust clouds from the far side of the earth.

On the lawn outside the courthouse stood the magistrate, MacKenzie. He was pointing with his riding crop at the Japanese flag on the flagpole, and bellowing some sort of gibberish in the direction of the arid harbour, as though there were someone out there whom no one but him could see.

Madness, Grimaldi muttered: that old fool was just as bad as Amelie. Why couldn't people be more logical? Why were they always dreaming up these scatterbrained notions? If it wasn't old man MacKenzie with his invisible Japanese Navy, it was his dingbat of a wife with her premonitions, with her visions of a God who had given up on the world. If only they could be as rational as he was: that would obviously solve all their problems. Logic: that was everything, the cornerstone of civilization. It was a love of pure science and logic that had lead the young Grimaldi to pursue a career in the medical profession. Bringing health to the human body was a simple matter of establishing order, hacking away all the unruly bits and coaxing what was left into line. It was exactly the same sense of order that had allowed his British ancestors to civilize this barbaric coastline, building perfect little replicas of Edwardian English hamlets, complete with flagpoles bearing fluttering Union Jacks and whitewashed Anglican churches, and slapping them up on desolate cliffs to be pounded by the

111

merciless storms. That isolated village on the edge of the cruel Pacific, washed up a hundred years ago by the rising tide of empire, was, in Grimaldi's mind, an emblem of all that was good and clean and British. And bedamned if any unseasonal tide was going to shake his faith in *that*.

Heartened, Grimaldi scrambled the remaining distance up the hillside, batting the thistles aside with his umbrella as if they were groups of impertinent patients. Striding up the driveway past the rusted-out DeSoto, his cougar hounds pausing to piss on the tires and the stalks of the blighted Rhododendrons, the doctor had to shield his eyes against the blazing light reflected from the glass doors and picture windows. It looked as if the whole house were in the throes of some sort of spontaneous combustion, as if the wood and glass were burning with some mysterious inner flame. Pulling back the wide French doors, he stepped into the gloom of the parlour, as hesitant as a diver plunging into a shadowy pool.

Blinded for a moment by the darkness of the parlour, Grimaldi hovered helplessly just inside the doorway, groping for the familiar shapes of Amelie's Victorian armchairs. His dogs almost bowled him over as they romped toward the hallway, their clawed feet scrabbling wildly at the dusty hardwood floors. As his surroundings swam back into focus, he picked his way through the clutter of footstools and spindly-legged tables, ignoring the glass orbs and cups full of tea leaves, the Ouija board with its counter like a tiny grand piano, the volumes of Nostradamus bound in apocalyptic crimson, the chess game left unfinished on some long-forgotten summer evening, and proceeded to search as methodically as his drunkenness allowed him through every room in the maze of rooms in that endless, unoccupied house.

Amelie's scent was everywhere, like the scent of musk in a cedar forest, and her flimsy, scarcely real possessions seemed to have arranged themselves on every conspicuous surface, as if she had left them there as keepsakes before departing from this world. But there was no sign of the woman herself, or of her dark twin, The Other Amelie. In every room the doctor went, he was met by a brooding silence. The bedrooms blazed with ethereal light and the halls were as dark as tunnels. Grimaldi's suits hung like sloughed-off skin in the closets of his private chambers. The ghost of the drowned maid was humming in the kitchen, peeling her fingers as if they were carrots, her hair full of blanched leaves and pale, downy feathers. In the bedroom, Amelie's Tarot cards lay sprawled across the dust-furred carpet, as if a wind had blown through the doctor's life and his fate had come unravelled.

Having finally come full circle, Grimaldi found himself back in the parlour. Flopping gracelessly into one of the high-backed chairs, he gazed absently into the shadows, transfixed by a vague sense of purposelessness, his need for a drink having slipped from his mind. On the opposite wall of the room was a mirror, a gleaming ellipse of burnished glass in a frame of sculptured metal. In its depths, he could see himself standing on a shore, at the edge of an endless ocean. The waves rolled in from the far side of the world, the wind was keening, the sea birds shrieked, the rain angled down all around him. In the distance, he could see the two Amelies in a boat; they were waving and twirling their parasols. A rusty, bulbous submarine had surfaced through the spume; on its foredeck stood the magistrate, MacKenzie. In the village, far above him, he could hear the people cheer. A marching band was playing *Rule Brittania*.

Picking himself up from the high-backed chair, Grimaldi staggered over to the mirror on the wall, in which the images he'd seen or dreamed were already fading into mist, as lost as the life that he had thought that he was living. There was nothing in the mirror, when he got there, but an old man's face as worn and lined as driftwood in the ocean, eroded by the relentless scouring of the tide. Then even that had vanished, and the glass was clear and shining, a sea of light as vast as all the oceans in the world.